Penguin Books
August is a Wicked Month

Edna O'Brien was born in the West of Ireland
and now lives in London with her two sons.
She has written *The Country Girls*, *Girl with
Green Eyes*, *Girls in their Married Bliss*, *August is
a Wicked Month*, *Casualties of Peace*, *The Love
Object* (short stories), *Night*, *A Pagan Place*,
Zee and Co, *A Scandalous Woman and Other Stories*,
Mother Ireland, *Johnny I hardly knew you*,
Arabian Knights (with photographs by Gerard
Klijn) and *Mrs Reinhardt and Other Stories*. *The
Collected Edna O'Brien*, containing the nine novels,
was published in 1978 and *Some Irish Loving*, an
anthology of prose and poetry, in 1979.
Edna O'Brien was awarded the *Yorkshire Post*
Novel Award in 1971.

Edna O'Brien

August is a Wicked Month

Penguin Books

Penguin Books Ltd, Harmondsworth,
Middlesex, England
Penguin Books, 625 Madison Avenue,
New York, New York 10022, U.S.A.
Penguin Books Australia Ltd, Ringwood,
Victoria, Australia
Penguin Books Canada Ltd, 2801 John Street,
Markham, Ontario, Canada L3R 1B4
Penguin Books (N.Z.) Ltd, 182–190 Wairau
Road, Auckland 10, New Zealand

First published by Jonathan Cape 1965
Published in Penguin Books 1967
Reprinted 1967, 1968, 1970, 1971, 1973, 1975,
1976, 1977, 1978, 1979

Set, printed and bound in Great Britain by
Cox & Wyman Ltd, Reading
Set in Monotype Baskerville

for Stanley Mann

He has his winter too of pale misfeature,
Or else he would forgo his mortal nature.

Chapter One

The weather bureau forecast sun. It was not mistaken·
All day for five days it sizzled in the heavens and down
below the city of London simmered. People who had
hoped for summer wished now for a breeze and a little
respite. Only at night did Ellen feel cool. Watering the
garden and then sitting in the stone alcove. Provident
stone. It gave back the warmth taken throughout the hot
day and she saw it as something human – the mother who
reserves love for when it is most needed. She often sat for
an hour, caressing the stone, listening for the sounds of
her child if he happened to be sleeping in her house, listening anyhow, which is what one does alone at night in a
garden hushed by darkness. It was the best hour, sitting
there, warmed, and calm, and a little sad. But next day
it would be boiling again. The child's father decided
that they would go into the country. They would camp
out he said, and make fires and go fishing and do things
the boy wanted to do. It only took a day to get the
various necessaries and they were ready to leave on
Thursday.

In the shade end of the kitchen they sat, drinking tea,
she from her mug, he from the blue china cup reserved for
guests; hardly speaking. Through the glass half of the
kitchen door they watched their child, putting up the tent
in the garden. It was already fixed on two poles, a bright
blue, flapping back and forth like a flag. The father had

done that bit and now the child was putting the pegs in, and giving instruction to George.

'Well into the ground, George,' the child said. George was nobody. The child invented him three years before when he was five. It happened that a George came to visit them but very quickly got bored with a child of five and made an excuse about having to go home because of a pain in his head. But the child kept conversing with him after he'd left and held on to him throughout the years.

'It's a beautiful blue,' she said, looking through the glare of the sun as the child pulled on a rope and the canvas bellied out.

'They undercharged me,' her husband said, piling sixpences, shillings and two-shilling pieces in separate banks on the table, reckoning what he had paid for the tent, the fittings and the two Lilos. Always slow at adding, he reckoned things up when he got home and for some reason he was invariably undercharged. 'Because of his contemptuous face,' she thought, 'because he frightened shop girls and set them astray in their tottings and possibly one or two of them would think him attractive.'

'I got away with nine and elevenpence,' he said.

'You want me to take it back?' she asked.

'Nonsense.' He despised petty honour, but no longer thought it his duty to correct this or any other flaw in her.

'Look,' she said and pointed. The tent had swollen out now and as the child pulled on the last bit of rope it rose like a cone of bright blue towards the sky where the light was fiery.

'He's a strong child,' she said, 'to be able to do it.'

'I believe in teaching him these things,' her husband said, jumbling the various coins together and putting them in the pocket of his jacket which was spread over the back of his chair. Once when visiting her he hung his jacket on a nail and she went through the pockets for clues, reverting

8

to wifedom again. He must have known. He kept his jacket close to him ever since and picked it up and took it with him even on the short journey through the scullery to the outside lavatory.

'Anything you want for your trip?' she said, guiltily. No, he'd seen to everything. In the boot of the car there was tinned food, Primus stove, sleeping-bags, seedless oranges, Elastoplast, disinfectant and various medicines which he'd transferred through a funnel from big economy bottles to littler bottles, suitable for packing. He was far-seeing, careful and exigent. There was nothing left for her to contribute but a tin of shortbread.

'You could come with us,' he said flatly as she got out the shortbread and assured him untruthfully that it was home-made. Still cowering. She shook her head to his invitation. It needed a less insipid approach than that to bring her back. They'd separated two years before and the child was shared between their two homes. Out of necessity he invented George. They'd got over the worst part; the acrimony when she first left and when he posted broken combs, half-used compacts and old powder puffs in his campaign to clear out her remains. They'd got over that and settled down to a sort of sullen peace, but they talked now as she always feared they might, like strangers who had never been in love at all.

'He's calling us,' she said, relieved to escape. The child was saying, 'Mama, Dada, Dada, Mama,' in a shrill and happy way. She went out and raptured over the tent and said what a genius he was.

'Now you can take it all down,' his father said soberly. He'd got the child to put it up as an exercise.

'I'll help you,' she said, kneeling down not so much to help as to get nearer to him, to kiss his clean hair and touch his cheek and take full advantage of the last few minutes of contact. He would love her to join them. He would hug her and say, 'Good old Mama,' but she couldn't. Anyhow she consoled herself with the thought that he was happy. If she went there would be gloom and she could not bear the thought of night and her husband appointing their sleeping positions – he and her at either end of the new Lilos, the child in between, tossing and turning in the heat. For the last year of their marriage he avoided her in bed and she did not ever want to re-live that. The days would be testy – no music, no telephone, no floor to sweep, nothing to fill in the hours of treachery between them. She could not go.

'You'll write me sloppy letters,' she said to her son.

'Not sloppy,' he said, as he uprooted the pegs, flushed from work and self-importance. Still giving orders to George.

At exactly four minutes to three they set off. She looked down at her watch to appear practical. The sun had gone behind a cloud and the sunshine fell in a spray over the grey motor as they drove away with the child in the back seat squeezed in between a lot of luggage. His father always put him in the back seat in case of accident.

'Goodbye, goodbye,' the small hand on the window delivering kisses. The fingers on the glass tapping. The face wrinkled up because it was embarrassed and might also cry.

'Goodbye, goodbye.' She could hardly keep her eyes on them.

She came in the house, picked up the underpants and vest that the child had peeled off, held them, looked at them, smelt them, and finally washed them and hung them out to dry. Then she sat at the kitchen table, and put her face on her arm. The sandals he'd discarded were on the table. A prong missing in the buckle of one. His father said to keep them, they might come in useful. They might or they might not. She sat there, feeling, out of habit, for the missing prong, her head on her arm, her arm wet from crying, darkness coming on again. The silver fish that had got in with a grocery order were darting over the floor in search of crumbs and spilt sugar.

'Goodbye, goodbye.' They were a long way off now; they might even have pitched tent and settled in for the night, the child fast asleep, the father sitting outside, breathing and gratified, a tarpaulin spread on the grass, because of the dew. He liked the country and was a very light sleeper.

Chapter Two

A week later she could afford to laugh at that night of monstrous loneliness. As she said to herself, leaning over the garden wall, 'Something always comes, out of the blue.' A taciturn male companion stood next to her and the interlude would have been perfect except that the loose sand along the top of the wall grazed her bare arms. They had been there for over an hour now and she was weary of holding herself straight, which was why she resorted to leaning at all. Different for him because his jacket sleeves protected his elbows. At regular intervals either one put a hand up and rescued the rug that they shared from slipping away. They wore it as a shawl over their shoulders because he said there was dew falling. It seemed beneficent as he said it, the dew that they could not see falling softly upon them, like mercy. There would be dew in Wales falling upon her husband and son. They got there. She'd had one card. The child wrote the greeting, the father the address. The greeting said 'We are in a field with cows,' and there were a lot of kisses and not enough room left for his name so that he only signed three letters of it. The cows would gather around the tent, she thought, and stare in at them. The after-grass would not be too high either, because of the cows keeping it cropped. And milk easy to buy. In the dark the cows would settle under the trees coughing and wheezing, and the child would fall asleep to that unfamiliar soothing sound and the watchful father would keep watch. Very early in the morning he might even dreg a mug of illicit milk for their breakfast before the farmer came to round up the cows for their real milking. The milk would be warm in the mug at first but cool by the time he had boiled the kettle and made the tea. The child loved tea and took three spoons of sugar, and dipped his crusts when there was no one authoritative looking.

It was the first evening that she did not miss them desperately. But that was because she had company.

From her back garden they stood and looked at the lights reflected in the River Thames. The river ran by at the end of the garden. An enviable position. Cloaked by the rug and close together they looked in exactly the same direction, towards the water at three sets of lights: silver lights forming six silver pipes in the water, their shadows behind them and a little to one side, then in the centre were the gold pipes of light like golden pillars in a church, and to the far right were black-green ones, the colour of porter bottles. There were many other things to be seen in London that night, Bovril signs and a moon and the bulky outline of a round gasometer, but they chose to look only at the pipes of light that swooped in a half-circle from left to right at that point where the river curved and went on towards distant Battersea and possibly created other images for other intending lovers.

'If it were a painting we would try to explain it,' he said.

'We try to explain everything,' she said.

In fact he talked less than anyone she'd ever been with before. They both said so little that they heard every sound, even the preparatory flaps of a duck before it took off in flight.

'A duck has been molested,' she said. He sighed. Was he bored?

'No, I breathe shallowly. I sigh all the time.'

'Which must be beautiful for those near you,' she said, and then apologized for the train noise going by. She'd become used to it. He did not mind.

'Our frog is making progress,' he said. A frog was on its way to the pond in the centre of the garden. It had come out from under the unwieldy hedge a while before and its moves though sudden were barely perceptible, and these moves and his shallow breathing and the river going by and the dew – she had to take his word for this – falling, gave a slowness to the evening as if every second was being lengthened and they were aware of everything going on. The whole day had been slow like that and perfectly so.

'He's almost there,' he said. He had turned round to observe the frog's progress and now he faced the river again and gave the rug a little pull so that it was secured again. She felt him moving nearer and then their hips touched and they stayed like that, not agitating each other, just getting closer as they looked across the river and downwards at the pipes of light. In time their arms locked and their shoulders rubbed as if they were witching one another. His hand came around her waist and the rug began to slip because they put their remaining hands – her two and his one – to love uses, tracing each other's faces, touching, lingering, drawing away, feeling a lip's thickness, finding out. She was glad now that her arms were bare because his touch brought them to life with one sort of move, then another.

'They're singing,' she said, 'my arms are.' Rusted from disuse they began to come to life. Ripples of pleasure running down the length of those bare, white, rusted arms.

'So you made your own candles,' she said. 'At Christmas.' He'd told her earlier on that they'd melted white candles at Christmas time and put cochineal in them and had candles with ribs of colour running through them. *They.*

'What makes you think of that?' he said.

'The colours running through them, the way there's ripples running through me now.' She wished he had a thousand hands and could bring all of her body to life at the same moment. He was doing what he could. Her arms were singing and her hips wild with little threads of joy running through her like little madnesses. After a year's solitary confinement.

'I'm out of practice,' she said.

'A girl like you.' He didn't believe it. Who would? She was twenty-eight and had skin like a peach and was a free woman with long rangy legs and thick, wild hair, the colour of autumn.

'At times,' she said, 'I longed to be touched but you can't go and ask people, you can only ask yourself.'

'Yourself?' he said.

'Yes,' she said, sadly.

'That's bad,' he said.

He caught the rug just as it slipped on to the wet grass and with both hands he brought it up behind his back, and over his shoulders, to his head.

'Have I shocked you?' she said. He smiled forgiveness, and then stretched the rug forward to cover her head, and when both their heads were engulfed by the rug he let go of it and he put his arms round her and took her mouth and felt it at first with his outer lips and then with the inside of those lips which was far softer. Their tongues wound round and round in a perfect, dizzying rhythm and he told her to open her mouth wide and wider. She received him right back the length of her mouth to her taste buds and although she feared choking she also thought she was sampling some beautiful fruit she had never known before. Her bones were singing away and the taste in her mouth was of magic. When they needed to breathe he lifted the rug back and put it like a veil around his face, and they were free to breathe for a minute and to watch. His face was good; pale, languid, and happy now. He normally looked bored. He had good bones and a habit of moistening his upper lip with his tongue all the time. To smile he had to do very little. He smiled so gently, so exquisitely and yet his face was not ever broken up into a big vulgar crease. He smiled around the eyes and there were plenty of lines there. Maybe he smiled a lot.

'Why did you come?' she asked, having put the question aside all day. He'd come at eight that morning and she'd gone down in a long-sleeved nightdress with an uneven hemline to answer the door thinking that it was the postman with a parcel or a registered letter. There he stood in a dark suit, an irreproachably white shirt and dark glasses. It took her several seconds to recognize him because she'd only seen him once.

'Am I too early?' he said.

'Come in,' she said and ran up the stairs before he could see her nightdress. She put on a girdle and a suit and then came down and shook hands with him formally and offered him breakfast. She thought it odd that he should have come, and she thought it improper that she should be frying him bacon and eggs without having panties on. She felt the coolth of her thighs and thought it nice to feel her own coolness and her distance from this man who'd obviously come because he was in some sort of trouble. Only trouble could have brought him out at that hour, braving the world in a pair of dark glasses. He stayed all day, slept in the garden on the rug that she'd taken off her bed and trailed down the stairs. He drank gins and tonic with six cubes of ice per drink and he was so fanatical about the ice that he filled the twelve-sectioned metal tray with water and turned the clock to full freezing speed so that more ice would be available through the course of his drink.

'Why do you think I came?' he said.

'Trouble?' But she was happy about it.

'Miranda,' he said, 'has become my lodger. I've got a lodger who won't go.'

'You'll have to get spades in,' she said, and thought how quickly high love wanes. Miranda was his mistress. Ellen had met them both a year before, Miranda somebody and this pale distant man who talked to her for a few minutes and asked what she did. She said that she worked for a little theatre magazine and had been married once and didn't approve of it and had a son. They got on to marriage. He'd been married too. He had hordes of children and a washed-out wife. But Miranda was calling.

'Yes, darling.'

'Mashed potato dance.' She had her arms out to welcome him. She was a tall girl with an abundance of hair. Birds could nest in it. She'd had it dyed various grey-green woodland colours and she looked very womanly as she held her arms out and drew him near her. Miranda someone. The man who gave the party said she was dull and talked about Fallopian tubes all the time. Ellen felt relieved because the odds would have been too heavy if her temperament measured up to her handsome face and her lovely woodland hair. She did not talk to him again that night except that he came to say goodbye when he was leaving. He rang her at her office a few days later to tell her about a woman who put rubber bands instead of bacon rinds on her mousetraps, and to ask, incidentally, how she was. She said she was well and dashing off somewhere – which she was – and he asked what she was wearing and she said a brown dress with chiffon sleeves and amber beads and washed hair, which was true.

'You would,' he said churlishly, meaning he envied whoever it was she was going to see, and she guessed that he must have some interest in her in so far as a man with four children, a deserted wife, and a mistress can have the luxury of giving a thought to another woman. That was over a year before. For a few days or weeks she went around thinking of him and suffering, but the ache trickled away like all her other false-alarm aches, and when he arrived in dark glasses she was shocked to think that for a certain time he had burnt holes in her thoughts.

'You're sorry I came. I bore you,' he said.

'Not really. We had a nice dinner. I mightn't have stirred myself to cook otherwise.' She had her summer vacation from the office and was in the habit of going out to the café for a snack in the evenings. Without her son, or without a guest, she found that cooking saddened her. Alone, she ate standing up, so as not to make a ceremony of it.

'And what now?' he said. He'd put the rug over them again and they resumed kissing.

'Like the last time,' he said.

'I've never opened it so wide before,' she said.

'In that case I ought to bring you to bed and teach you all my wicked ways.' The first and in fact the only funny thing he said. They moved up the garden and climbed the terrace of steps to the room that overlooked the river.

'You're lucky to be loaned this house.' A rich woman who'd gone off to Africa had loaned her the house for a year.

'I'm always lucky,' she said, leading the way to her bedroom. He said they did not need the light on and she in turn asked if he would like the curtains drawn.

'Leave them open,' he said. 'We'll see the sun in the morning.'

'Who said there will be sun?' Relief. She thought, he means to stay until morning, and that pleased her as much as that he was going to sleep with her. She remembered a man who got up and left straight after he came, while she was still in the throes of desire.

In bed she opened wide. And christened him foxglove because it too grew high and purple in a dark secretive glade. He put the bedside light on. She felt him harden and lengthen inside her like a stalk. Soft and hard together. He loved her as no man had ever done, not even the husband who first sundered her and started off the whole cycle of longing and loving and pain and regret. Because that kind of love is finally emptying.

'You loved me lovely,' she said. His back was bathed in sweat. He had laboured on her behalf and she was filled with the most inordinate gratitude.

'I'll cool it,' she said, dipping her hand in the water jug and spreading it over his back to mix with his sweat in a cool balm. Then he lay on his back and said good night although he was already asleep.

In the crook of his arm she lay and listened to him snore. She did not mind him snoring. She felt too happy to sleep. She just lay there thinking about nothing at all except that she was happy.

'Say you're sorry,' she said in the morning when he wakened and blinked at the light pouring in and looked around the strange room and then at the unfamiliar red hair spread over the pillow, next to him. She was saying it as a joke and to forestall him.

'Say I'm sorry!' he said. 'For what?'

'Just in case you are,' she said.

'Are you?'

'No I'm happy.'

'I'm dumbfounded,' he said. 'I can't believe it. I met you once.'

'Twice,' she said, 'including yesterday. But never without pounds of stuff on my face.'

He liked her face better like that. Without its mask.

And he loved her again and spoke very little except to say how sweet it was.

They had breakfast and sat in the garden until it was time for her luncheon appointment. More sunshine. He dozed and talked a little and wondered aloud what he would do.

'I suppose I'll have to move out,' he said. 'It's so bloody unfair, the man always has to leave.'

'Not always,' she said, thinking of her own situation and how she'd left and had to fend for herself.

'I suppose I can't ask her to leave,' he said.

There was so much that Ellen wished to say and so much that she wanted to ask but she said nothing for fear of jeopardizing her chances with him. She hid all her meannesses and gave him a drink weighed down with ice cubes. They sat supporting each other with their backs, sometimes one or other of them hummed a song that was very popular at that time, called 'Anyone who had a heart', and the words were especially nice because of the way they were feeling. At noon he offered to drive her to the centre of London.

'Why are you smiling?' he said as they stopped and started. It was Saturday and the traffic was bad.

'Why?' she said, lightly. So much had happened. She felt new again. Soft and indulgent towards the bad-tempered traffic. Looking at his ear lobe she remembered and told him how a drop of sweat behind it, in bed, had the effect of a crystal about to drop off. She kept moving from one position to another to give all her limbs a lovely stretch.

'You have so much energy,' he said.

'I'm just boisterous.' He looked at her and smiled and then looked in the car mirror and smiled to himself. He was happy too.

'It's not every day one gets a gift and gives a gift,' she

said. She wanted to do something lovely and loving for him. To give him a garden in full bloom – he liked flowers and was cultivating daisies in window-boxes – or a stone with a thousand colours, something he would never want to discard. Mainly she talked and hugged herself with happinesses, and twice when they were held up at the lights he kissed her. She knew they would meet again and she did not have to press him about when or where.

'I suppose we'll ring each other up,' he said when she got out and stood on the kerb holding the door.

'I suppose we will,' she said. Wise now with the soft lustre of love upon her. Her eyes shining. They would meet soon and she would open again. The river of his being flowing into the pasture of her body. She was thinking of that when she got to the restaurant.

Chapter Three

Which made the lunch boring. A stingy theatre producer asking her what plays he ought to put on. Her. A week before she might have found it flattering. This well-known face with its striped suit and Mexican silver cuff-links at a special table near the window, some actress somewhere trying to catch his eye. He'd brought her to the roof garden of the hotel and they sat looking at the monstrosities of London: buildings jumbled in together and the appearance from up above of there being practically no trees and only one dusty parkland in the maze of un-matching houses and narrow streets.

'So you haven't found the perfect man yet?' he said.

'No, but I've applied for one.' He tasted his cold soup. It was not chilled enough. He beckoned. The waiter who came over spoke no English, but lifted the bowl of thick soup out of its ice bed to show that it ought to be chilled enough. Her friend argued that it wasn't, and that the pure orange juice they'd ordered was not pure but tinned. She had a feeling that they were being looked at. The waiter was having his revenge. She was wasting time.

'And what will you do with your life?' he said, waiting for the second bowl of soup to be brought.

'I'll just be,' she said. A rare thing for her, racked as she was with anxiety, wondering always what would happen next, if an affair would be eternal, or if she loved her son over much, or if the wheels of a car they sat in would fly off and leave them half dead on the roadside.

'So you're getting sensible,' he said.

'I'm getting old.' Not for years had she felt happier, more content, and therefore youthful. The bill was high and he left in a surly humour.

That evening she waited in and read a little (Keats) and walked around and journeyed to the end of her garden to make certain that the pipes of light were still there. She put a stone to the door in case she missed the ringing of the telephone. The evening was very still and the sound carried perfectly, so that in fact she heard the very first ring it gave as she ran up the lawn, past the frog pond and leapt up the steps. For some reason that had nothing to do with her running the necklace she wore dismantled and the beads ran down the steps as she was running up but it did not matter.

'Hello,' she said, as she picked up the phone and tried not to sound as if she'd hurried.

'Can you come and have a drink?' It was not him at all, but another man who often rang her on the spur of the moment to ask her out.

'I can't,' she said. 'There's someone coming here.'

'Infidelity,' he said. He liked her a little and she often said to him how unfortunate that she could not have love affairs with someone for whom she had affection. Fear and hatred were what motivated her passions.

'I hope he's a dwarf,' he said.

'He's almost,' she said, and promised to have a drink another time and rang off.

Then she went to collect up the spilt beads. Some were easy to find, but as it got dark she trained the beam of a flashlamp into the corners of the mossy steps and felt with her fingers for the tiny pearled ones that were strung between the big blue beads and middle-sized glass ones. It was important to find every bead, not just to repair the necklace but because she took it as an omen. When she had retrieved a pile she held them between her palms, tossing them from one hand to another, killing time, and every so often she put her hand down and in the dark found another in a corner or under a weed. It was funny how you could go on finding them. Later she came in the house and sat in front of the telephone, staring at it, waiting for it to come to life, hoping, beseeching, lifting it from time to time to make sure it was not out of order, then, relieved at its regular purr she would drop it suddenly in case he should be dialling at that very moment, which he wasn't.

Late next evening she took it upon herself to ring him. He worked at night in a newspaper office, writing editorials.

'I don't know why *I'm* ringing,' she said chirpily. He asked how she was and what she'd done. She lied a bit about having gone out a lot and said her necklace was all over the garden, and then she heard herself say, softly and shamelessly, 'It was lovely with you.'

He said yes and how he hadn't been so happy for years and how he regretted nothing.

'And?' she said.

'I just don't know,' he said. 'I love Miranda as I keep finding out every time I leave and come back to her. I suppose I want it every way, and I have such ...' He meant guilt, problems, responsibilities, but could find no single word to contain his meaning. He said they would meet in a while and she knew that possibly they would but it would be a duty meeting out of courtesy.

'You're all right?' he said. 'I mean, not worried?'

'Not very,' she said. She would have to resign herself to being alone again, alone like she was the previous morning when he came for comfort, except that now she'd lost that spacious calm that had been here through months of training, of discipline, and abstinence, and doing work and loving her child and watering the garden.

'I think you're one of the nicest people I ever met,' he said. And meant it.

'You too,' she said, and they said a few more nice things and then they had to ring off because his other telephone was buzzing. It was no lie, she could actually hear the buzzing.

'People get what they deserve,' she said as she came off the phone. A great believer in punishment. She wondered if he'd told Miranda where he'd been.

The next couple of days were bad. She went around the house in her nightdress, thinking of him, thinking of her son, and the holiday that she'd meant to have. It had been her intention to walk around London and become a sort of tourist doing tourist things like taking a bus into the country and gathering leaves or buying bits of pottery to bring home. The fear that he might not ring was so great that she had to take the telephone off the rest to remove all possibility of his ringing, but part of her kept putting it back on again and hoping. She drank a lot and two nights she went to bed drunk and her head swam and the mattress swooned and she lay with the curtains open.

On the third day she went out to buy food. It was dull for August. A haze hung over the street and it was uncertain whether the sun would shine or if there would be rain. People were downcast.

'We haven't had a summer,' the greengrocer said, forgetting about the five days. She bought strawberries to cheer herself up.

'You're going away?' he said. She said no, but was he? He said later he'd go to Spain with the sister and they'd eat maggots and drink vino and come home tanned.

'It's astonishing,' he said, 'the way the sun gets you. Like the devil, that's it, it's demonic, like the devil. You've

25

been around, you know what I mean. You get that you want it, irresistible . . .'

'I know what you mean,' she said as she went on her way up the High Street, past the flower stall and past the man who held up and acclaimed plastic wardrobes but sold none and towards the bookshop where she intended to get a new book to distract herself. She would sit on the bench at the top of the High Street and read a bit and watch the people go by and look at the big public house across the way which said 'BANQUETS, RECEPTIONS' and maybe the Cypriot would be there. He came most days. A big sad hulk of a man with a simpleton for a sister. They smiled at each other and once when he was eating an orange he tore off a section and gave it to her.

She had never noticed a tourist office in that place but now she saw one down a side street, about four doors from the corner. She went to look in the window and saw a coloured photograph of two girls in straw hats under a beach umbrella smiling to receive someone who was not shown in the photograph. The girls wore purple bikinis and their bellies were chocolate coloured with the belly button beautifully concave and she thought of him again and how the second time they had made love towards morning, he had not come inside her at all but touched her with his body, finding new places of pleasure that were virgin, and she longed for him as she stood in the street and thought the wickedest thing he had done was to come like that and give her false hope, and renew her life for an evening when she had resigned herself to being almost dead. Who, going by with prams and shopping and punnets of strawberries leaking blood, would know that she stood at a window with aggravation between her legs? It was demonic like the greengrocer said, and looking up at the overcast sky she cursed it for its darkness and cursed her own dark, convent life. She had been brought up to believe in punishment; sin in a field and then the long awful spell in the Magdalen laundry scrubbing it out, down on her knees getting cleansed. She longed to be free and young and naked with all the men in the world making love to her, all at once. Was that why he ran? He saw jail written all over her face. And punishment. And looking again towards the window she said aloud, 'I'll punish him, I'll go away,' because of course she still hoped he would have another row with Miranda and come back for her. She went into the shop not knowing what she intended to inquire about. A delicate young man, who badly needed sun, told her there were dozens of places to go and gave her a free booklet to consult. She sat at a table and opened it at a page that said, 'France will prove an adventure in all that is pleasurable in existence', and she saw photographs of beaches beautifully fronded by palm trees and she remembered a novel set on a French beach where all people though decadent were touched with a special, mellifluous charm. And she went back to the young man, with the page open. He'd been there himself once with his fiancée and its marvels had to be seen to be believed.

'Breathtaking,' was his word for it.

'Do people go there on their own?' she said. 'I mean women?'

'Best way to go,' he said. She thought she heard regret in his voice. Had he wanted to slip away for an evening and have some lunatic encounter on that beach under one of those incredibly tall trees?

She would go there.

'The sooner the better,' she said as he rang up to arrange a flight and book an hotel. Her husband and son would not be back for a week or more and she would lie in a strange new place and let strange new things happen.

Afterwards she went to buy clothes. She bought

trousers and shirts with slits at the sides to be worn over trousers and gold sandals with a strap separating the big toe from the other toes. Freedom clothes.

'Do you know, I've never worn trousers,' she said to the shop assistant. Squeamishness. As children they'd been told all that. And not to cross their knees because it caused Our Lady to blush. Well she was getting fast clothes now and blue trousers and Our Lady could blush to her follicles.

'Slacks suit you,' the assistant said. She had another pair over her arm, of lighter material, suitable for evenings. Ellen was overspending, but she told herself that she would skimp when she got back and do extras for the magazine throughout the winter, like reviewing out-of-town plays that no regular reviewer would deign to go to. She took the second pair as well. They were of green silk with a coatee to match. A small division between the waistband of the trousers and the end of the coatee. An inch of stomach showing, white as milk.

At home she fitted the new clothes on again and packed them in a case as she took them off. She painted her toe-nails carmine and pared the two corns on her little toes and thought them almost decorative like pearls, with their hard white centres. She danced in the new green outfit to wireless music. Dancing alone now, but by the same time next day she would be walking down a path to the sea, languid because of the heat, and she would stand and throw something in the water and know that there was some stranger behind, shadowing her, smiling and when she turned they . . . . She was happy and breathed deeply, deeply. But for him she might never have gone. 'Bless you, Hugh Whistler,' she said, as she copied the exact address of the newspaper so that she could send him back a snappy, happy, I-don't-give-a-damn-about-you postcard. She ironed her son's clothes and put them in a pile on his bed for when they all got back and life was normal again. She stored his sandals away. She did exercises to be supple and wrote the milkman a note. She packed odds and ends of food in a cardboard box and left them to a woman down the street. She could not sleep. In the mirror, as she danced with the portable radio, she saw herself in the new clothes with the milk-white waist showing and her toe-nails glistening, a wicked carmine in new gold sandals. She danced through the last night of aloneness. And when she slept it was in the downstairs room on a sofa with three alarm-clocks set to go off at intervals of five minutes each so that there was no possibility of her sleeping out. The flight was booked for noon.

Chapter Four

He looked at her twice but conveyed no emotion. He reminded her of certain men who played extras in French films; in that his face was long and thin and sharp featured. She purposely sat in the outside seat across the aisle from him because he was the best-looking man. She noticed him the minute they got in the aeroplane, while other people were settling down, fretting about the view, putting their hands up to control the air, pretending to be concerned about these things when in fact they were mainly terrified about being killed. They'd been flying for over an hour now and he'd stopped reading *France Soir*. He was looking around, mildly curious: at her, at the girl beside her with long hair and sloe eyes who had her sunhat placed on her lap like an ornament. Should she thank him? Say her ears were all right? When they took off she had developed a pain in them and panicked in case her swallow was going to cease, and the darts of pain through her ears were as if needles were being pushed through. He was the one to advise her to suck a sweet.

Could she discuss her ears – blobs of wax on the end of a hair-clip, deafness, the stink of bacteria? She looked through the window and tried to think of something subtle. The horizon was like a sandbank, only blue, with hollows in between the long blue crests and snow beyond that, or white sky. Pockets of cloud like phantom cloud moved over the fields; green fields and ploughed fields that were a dull, pinkish brown and the road was a river because of the way it wound in and out between the fields.

'The road is like a river,' she said, turning suddenly and catching his eye as he hitched up the leather belt around his waist. She could make love to him there and then, lie down and love this total stranger. She'd always wanted to. He had intelligent eyes. She was going to make overtures to every good-looking man she met. This trip was her jaunt into iniquity.

'*Pardon*,' he said. Oh God, to have to repeat it and be overheard by the girl with the sloe eyes.

'Just the road,' she said nervously. 'It reminds me of a river.'

'Good, good,' he said, smiling as if it were funny. She told him how she'd never been to France before and he predicted that she would find it mostly good.

'I don't even speak French,' she said.

'Many don't, but it still is mostly good.'

'I won't know what to do.'

'You will swim and sunbathe and eat good and perhaps gamble at night.' Was he proposing to do any of these things with her?

'You make it attractive,' she said, in a low voice.

'Yes, you will do all of these things for your holiday,' he said. He would have a holiday later in Italy, but now he must work. She told him where she was going and took out her diary to check on the name of her hotel.

'You know it?' she asked.

'No, I live many miles into the mountains. With my family.'

'Mountains,' she said lovingly, speculating not on their calm ineluctable beauty but on his life. There would be a wife and one or two small children and they would sit out of doors on a wall, waiting for him, the children drawing patterns in the dust with the sharp edge of a stone or a

31

slate that had come off the roof in winter, and there would be hens lazying around and perhaps a dog. The wife would knit, and her eyes would be calm, the calm contented eyes of a wife on a mountain with a husband coming home to love her.

'How do you get there?' she asked.

'I drive. I have my car at the airport since yesterday.'

'And there are buses also?'

'Buses. Yes.' He could see she was worried.

'I show you. I go the opposite way, otherwise I drop you, with pleasure.'

'Not at all,' she said, and looked away in case he should see the light go out of her face, her round face quenched in disappointment. She looked through the window again. They had passed the fields and were going over a mountain of grey stone. She stared down at the figurations of stone coiled together the way corpses would be and thought of death and how once as a child with her sister she lay in bed on a Saturday morning thinking of the day of general judgement and rehearsing the two possible alternatives that God would say: 'Depart from me ye cursed into everlasting flames which were prepared for the Devil and his angels,' or, 'Come ye blessed for my Father possesseth the Kingdom prepared for you,' and while they rattled off the words she was conscious of her father forcing her mother to submit and drawing the mother's face towards his with his hand under her chin and his thumb and forefinger dug into her, hurting her swallow and his other hand out of sight, doing something under the covers, and her mother resisting and saying 'Stop', while the children had first an argument and then a bet as to whether God would be up on a rostrum or not. At that time she approved her mother's resistance and now she felt differently: her mother should not have been mean, and she thought of making love again and turning to the stranger said, 'Perhaps you can come and eat with me one evening.'

'Perhaps,' he said, 'it will be possible,' and he smiled a sweet patient smile. Perhaps. Another silence.

Her first sight of the sea was of a saucer of deepest blue with patches around the edges. The patches were a turquoise and they looked as if they'd been put there specially. Like decoration. She gasped.

'It's perfect,' she said, as if he were responsible for it.

'I get the same answer from two ladies last week,' he said. He travelled over and back each week and she thought that if meeting him in France were impossible then she might still be able to meet him in London.

People began to gather themselves together, the dish of sweets came round again, more needles in her ears, the girl next to her putting on the sunhat and he opening a brief case and taking out a tie.

'I show you,' he said when she looked and wondered if he were about to vanish.

In fact he was vital at the air terminal because her suitcase was lost. He spoke to officials and gave her name and the name and telephone number of her hotel.

'Have a drink with me,' she said, really grateful.

'I make one telephone and I have a drink,' he said. She waited in the bar but he did not come back. Maybe she missed him when she went to do her face, or maybe it was the wrong bar. Anyhow she missed him. By the time she came down the bus had left for her destination and she decided to taxi. The price was posted up plain to see. Thirty New Francs. The driver was chatty, wide awake and merry. The merry eyes of an assassin. She felt light in the head, wide awake and ravenous to see. The palm trees were not trees at all but great green quills set into well-shorn barks, hardly swaying. No moss. No ivy. Nothing cluttered the bareness of the place. Pink and white houses of stone fast asleep in the afternoon sun with their shutters folded over and towels on balconies and water sprinklers wetting lawns. He drove very fast. Sometimes he spoke but she just shook her head or said something in English that caused him to shake his head, in turn. The light was dazzling. They came to a town and he pointed to an hotel with two flags overhead. It was on a hill with series of steps and grass terraces running down from it. Like a fairy tale house to which she was returning as in a dream. They drove right up the slope and under an open porch where he delivered her at the swing doors that were motionless. The agency had booked her safely, the assassin wished her well and by some extraordinary piece of mismanagement the air company had already delivered her lost case. She knew then that things were going to be all right. She signed the book and was given a key. She took the lift and then walked behind a bellboy who was carrying her heavy case down a corridor. She saw a naked man regarding her from a room. He held a door open a few inches and propositioned her not with a smile but with a look. He was in his thirties she estimated, and well built and the light in his room was dusk as if he had drawn the blinds and slept a bit and was now refreshed and ready for love. She looked at him and then hurried on for fear of losing the boy with the case. Her room was about ten doors farther down and on the opposite side to that of the naked man. It did not face the ocean. The brass bed was bigger than a single bed but nothing like a double. The bellboy put her bag on a straw stool and looked at her with a curious dazed expression and did not smile. The smell was strange. The clean, unfamiliar smell of linen and scouring powder and wood baked by the heat. The wood of the window-frame had many small cracks. It was a shabby room but nice. She unpacked straight away and hung her clothes up carefully, a dress for each hanger. She laid her muslin-light nightdress on the bed and said the word 'honeymoon'. There was a wash-basin and a bidet with a brownish stain around the faucet. A sign nailed above the wash-basin warned her about not drinking tap water. She picked up the telephone and very effusively asked for a bottle of Perrier.

'I've just arrived,' she said, partly as an apology and also to instigate a little welcome for herself.

The Perrier came in a tub of ice, like champagne. The boy who brought it was very affable. She over-tipped.

'Your name?' she asked.

'Hugo,' he said.

'Hugo.' He poured her drink, bowed, and left.

Out on the little balcony, wooed by the newness of the place, the town just beneath her, the silence, the sea somewhere, she stood sipping the drink, held by the sweet pressure of her thoughts, remembering vaguely: other smells, white frost on a road in Ireland, face powder in a glass bowl with a huge puff laid into it, the delicate mauve of a pigeon's breast; and comparing all these things with this new place that bore no resemblance to any other place she'd ever been to. The light was shattering. Her skin empty of colour. The dazzle on houses like metal. She stayed for over an hour. She thought of the man on the plane hitching up his leather belt and the naked one in the doorway, and the others everywhere about, waiting. She did not think of her son.

Chapter Five

By the time she got down to the hotel beach most of the mattresses were deserted. A few had the blemish of water where a wet body had recently lain, but mostly they looked like row upon row of dry, white, hospital beds. Beyond a railing was another beach and the mattresses there were striped. In the white sand all the footprints had effaced one another. She moved very cautiously and slunk on to a mattress when she thought the beach boy was not looking. Not meanness – she simply did not know how to ask for one. He was busy folding umbrellas and carrying them in bundles to a shed. He carried them like spears, their points forward, and stacked in the shed they looked like armour too. When he crossed over to talk to her she felt it an attack.

'*Anglais*,' she said, and started changing money in her head, setting herself quick sums so that she would be prepared no matter what amount he asked for. All he did was say the name of the hotel and then go off again. He was a dark, rich tan like everybody else in that place except herself and the English group a few mattresses away.

'Look at Arthur, he's turning,' a woman was saying, while her friends joined her in looking at an unfortunate specimen of a man who was raging pink.

'You'll have to wear shorts in the garden when you go home,' his wife said as she helped him to dress under a robe. She opened each leg of his underpants while he stepped into it and then she drew it up above his stomach and smoothed the cotton legs so that they did not bulge.

'All right, Arthur?' she said. He looked grumpy. Then he sat down while she put on his canvas shoes, worming each one over his swollen ankles with the help of a shoe-horn.

'Give him vinegar,' another woman said. She'd discovered its soothing properties the previous summer. She waved a bottle that seemed to contain a chocolate-coloured lotion.

'In a fancy bottle like that – vinegar?' Arthur's wife said. The woman had changed it into one of those sun-lotion bottles so that she wouldn't look foolish.

'Got it in Hull, on a beach. We went to Hull for our anniversary,' she said, proud of the bottle.

'Gladys is nothing if she's not economical,' a second man said and looked at her with bitterness. Once or twice they tried to engage Ellen by a word, or a mention of sun-burn or what it said in the English paper that day but she pretended not to notice. She sat upright and had her first view of the Mediterranean and thought it odd that it should mean nothing to her, nothing at all. She had more interest in looking at the beach boy as he swept the mat-tresses with the long, soft twig, but every time she looked in her direction the woman with the lorgnette had the eyeglass fixed on her. She was dressed in black and had a thick white snood over her hair. Between trying to avoid this woman and having to ignore the English group she found she had to keep looking in the direction of the sea. It was hazed over and she could not see to the far side. Then a young girl came and temporarily everything was changed.

They all stared because she moved so perfectly. She was in bare feet and her toes painted silver had the effect of having just had candle grease poured over them. They were so light compared with the rich, polished hues of her body. Like mahogany. The beach boy saluted her with the broom as she went by but she did not smile, her presence was its own reward. She came and sat two mattresses away from Ellen and lay right back trailing her hands in the warm sand. The woman with the lorgnette left Ellen abruptly and began staring at the new arrival. And then the man appeared. Almost on cue he stood on the balcony and looked down at the three people who were left. The English crowd had gone. He was like an advertisement for vigour. Gold-skinned with blond hair, and the spots of sand on his body gave him the glisten of stone. She thought he might be the one who propositioned her, naked, in the corridor but she could not be sure. In strange surroundings she could never identify faces and already the lift boy, the beach boy and the porter looked indistinguishable. He talked idly to another man but mainly he looked towards the beach. He looked at her and her heart machined as she saw his companion come down the steps and walk towards her. He was a fat man and he walked over daintily, treating the ground as a tightrope.

'*Mademoiselle?*' he said as he stood over her. She pretended to be puzzled. Then a sharp whistle from the balcony alerted them both and the golden sultan up above indicated to the fat man that he had made a mistake. Excusing himself, the fat man crossed over the bridge of mattresses to where the young girl lay.

'*Mademoiselle,*' he said. She must have been dozing because he had to say it twice and then she sat up somewhat startled.

'I hope you will forgive my intrusion but my friend would like to invite you to a party.'

'Your friend?' she said coldly. He pointed to the balcony and her eyes followed his finger. The man up above did not look at her for confirmation, but stared out to sea in the direction of a white fortress that was across the water. His castle.

'This evening, we are having a beach party,' the man said, over-humbly.

'I have another engagement,' the girl said. Ellen wished she could give answers like that instead of rushing to assignations with open arms.

'*Je suis désolé*,' the man said, and in English the girl asked why he had come.

'We are having a party on the beach, our biggest party,' he said.

'What time?'

'At nine, but we could have it later if you wish that.'

She said nothing for a minute and in the interval he took the opportunity to kneel on the sand. What tactics.

'You have another appointment?' he said again. She thought about it and said very realistically, 'I am going to the beauty parlour at eight.' Her hair was obscured by a green kerchief and she wore dark glasses that had rhinestones on their horn frames. There was no telling what effect the invitation had on her.

'Perhaps you could come after,' he said. She looked again at the man who was to be her escort and then she said that she would try to change her hair appointment. The fat man gave a slight nod towards the balcony and the sultan walked away, over-slowly. He walked well. He and the girl would make a perfect couple. Ellen felt the humiliation one feels in the presence of perfectly formed people and she had a moment's apprehension about having come at all. A child was laughing and saying '*Encore, encore,*' and she thought of her son.

'You are Swedish?' the man said, relaxing now with the girl and asking what she did for a living. She translated textbooks, which was why she spoke English, and then he asked how long she had been there.

39

'Three weeks,' she said.

'A beautiful girl like you and I haven't seen you before now.' His tone was flirtatious, but the girl retained her distance.

'Perhaps you have been on another beach?'

'No, this beach.' She was quite brisk. The sun, the opponent of dreams, had no place for subtlety, deceit, and the countless little looks that denote a passing attraction. A cauldron of honesty. Only the perfection people triumphed. The fat, the lame, the slobs, even the slightly blemished like Ellen would find it hard to pass as eligible. Unless of course she settled for the people in her own category. But who is willing to?

'I must be blind,' he said. The girl picked up her beach bag and rose to leave. She would see him later. He kissed her hand in an elaborate and theatrical way. Then he watched her walk away and when she had gone out of sight he caught Ellen's eye. He did not smile.

Soon there were only two people left, herself and the Lesbian. She was certain now that the woman in black was a Lesbian because of the way she kept holding the lorgnette and looking intense. Rather than have to talk to her Ellen left.

It was too early for dinner so she went back to her room and ordered tea. The same waiter as had brought the Perrier came and after she had tipped him he still stood there, beaming.

'*Parlez-vous français?*' he said.

'English,' she said.

'*Anglaise . . . ?*' he said. She nodded.

'*Ah Anglaise . . .*' he said triumphant. 'I fear I have mislaid my bus ticket.' He said it excitedly and laughed. They both laughed. The foolish laughter of strangers. She had to make it clear when she wanted him to leave.

Chapter Six

The dining-room had a terrace. White tables stretched from one end to the other, and beyond the tables the palm trees were visible. Yellow floodlights flared on the trunks of those suave trees and on the tables there were candles alight. The grease of seasons had thickened on the sides of the candlesticks. Every colour candle had burnt in those thick bottles, every colour grease had encrusted itself. She thought of his story about the cochineal and wondered if they would be friends at Christmas time and could she give him a present? She sat with an American doctor who had marginal diabetes. It meant he had to pick his diet most carefully.

'You come from?'

'England,' she said. She was tired of saying it and anyhow it was not true. But saying one came from Ireland resulted in tedious stories about fairies and grandmothers. He was a family man himself on a medical course. He was lonely.

'Don't get me wrong,' he said, 'I'm a happy man.'

The kids and the hamburgers meant everything.

'What about you?' he asked.

'I'm happy too,' she said and looked down at her wedding ring to hint. Might they go gambling later?

'Be my guest,' he said. She shook her head and tried to reply but a fish-bone had got in her throat. He gave her a crust and told her to chew it hard.

'Chew it,' he said, very loud. He chewed fiercely

to show what he meant. He was extremely coarse.

'Don't get me wrong,' he said. 'I just take the little lady out for the evening and we have fun.'

She looked at him with distaste.

'I'd hate to think you were getting the wrong impression. If I thought that I'd never speak to a strange woman again.' His eyes were beginning to anger. She kept looking down at her napkin where it had been darned. The darn was old and from various washings the thread was almost the same white as the linen.

'Let's see if you'll like it?' he said.

'Stop asking me,' she said suddenly. He snapped his hand then and called the waiter. A young boy came over and the American told him to cancel the order for dessert. The boy did not understand. The American repeated the command and left.

She kept her eyes on her plate for a while in case anyone else should engage her. But by nine o'clock everyone was seated and most people were half-way through. There was a feeling of agitation: pancakes burnt theatrically over flaming stoves, waiters talked angrily among themselves, overfull plates of soup just missed being bumped against, young boys knelt reverently to pick up a piece of cutlery that had fallen; and the diners talked and chewed with the savagery possible only in a strange public place where everyone else is talking and chewing as fiercely.

And as surely as they had all come, and debated over what to eat, and eaten it, so they all filed out again, sluggish now that they had been replenished. The main lights were turned down and the fever of the room began to subside. Waiters pushed trolleys of used dishes towards the kitchen and other waiters carried clean white cloths under their arms and set about restoring the tables. She was last.

It had fallen dark beyond the region of the diningroom. The light changed to ink without a dusk to forestall it. She'd eaten well. A raspberry seed had got caught in her tooth. Sitting there trying to worm it out, her eye fell on a man's jacket. It lay over a chair with the sleeves hanging down empty of arms. She longed to touch it because it was a dark velvet, the colour of plums in autumn. The colour of softness like the night, softness into which she longed to drown as into a pool or the pupils of large dark eyes. For some reason she recalled the velvet of soot at the back of a fireplace and her father singing 'Red River Valley', singing it affectedly in a nasal tone, and the neighbours listening politely and looking at the flames of the fire. It must have been Christmas, one of the few nice times. Her father was sober, her mother passed around plates of jelly and custard. The custard was thick. Then. Now the trees were stark. The night and the jacket were softness. But the trees still rose supreme, their trunks tall, the old palms whittled down to form a base around the new leaves and next year these new leaves would be whittled away too and the trees would be stronger still. She moved across and touched the jacket. She had many superstitions like that. As a child she had to touch certain stones in the walls on her way to school, and get to certain spots before counting twenty. The jacket felt nice and the smell of tobacco recalled being in the fierce embrace of a man. She stroked it slowly, the way she would stroke a curtain or a cat. The texture was soft and it smelt nice. Then she became aware of someone behind her. She turned sharply to apologize.

'I'm not a pickpocket,' she said.

A man stood before her in shirt sleeves. A tall man with dusky skin, and the smile of a baby. The whites of his eyes were immaculate like the clean table-cloths.

'I have not seen you before,' he said.

'I only arrived today,' she said, withdrawing from the jacket.

'You like it?'

'Yes, I like corduroy,' she said, and moved away. He put his hand out to detain her.

'You dance?'

'A little.' She should have taken a course in everything before coming to this place.

'I play the violin for you to dance.' He belonged to the orchestra that played for hotel visitors. He asked her to come in but explained that he would not be able to dance with her. She foresaw herself sitting by the wall, ignored, and the magic falling away from her like fake frosting or gold dust. She'd better not.

'A drink perhaps, later,' he said. How late? He did not finish until after midnight. She explained that she had just arrived and felt tired. No more impetuousness. There were ten long days to fill in.

'Tomorrow?' he said then.

'In the afternoon,' she said, conveying a certain morality. He had picked up her left hand and stared down at the ring on her marriage finger.

'Married?' he said.

'Once upon a time,' she said, trying to give the impression that a ring made no difference. They made a date for the following afternoon.

When he'd gone she went out and decided to take a stroll along the beach. Out in the lobby she had a slight moment of satisfaction. The perfect couple who had made the assignation on the beach were already at the disenchanted stage. The girl walked towards the lift, her head down. She looked totally different in clothes. Pert and secretarial, with her hair in an absurd bouffant. The fat man who had issued the invitation to her was behind, pleading, saying, 'You have some suspicion that is not so,' and the sultan was at the bar biting his thumb-nail. She looked at him now with reproach. Two men stared as she walked through the bar. The nursemaid outfit was effective and she looked like someone destined for the most poignant moment of the evening. In the garden the massed leaves made a fabric against the sky and there was a wind.

Among the palms were other trees that were taller and more feathery and these gave out a perfume. In the wind the perfume carried and got lost again and the sounds carried and faded like that too: foreign voices, arguments, a laugh, the syrup music of his violin trickling out. She went back to the beach where the mattresses were, not knowing any other walk just yet. It was totally empty, the mattresses like corpses. It was not lit up, but all around the lights of other hotels, and of the town and of nearby towns gleamed steadfast. The holiday night was happening. Under those lights people danced and walked and held on to each other, their senses heightened by the fairy-tale prettiness of the towns and the dark water with its withheld sea-sob: 'Ah . . . Ah . . . Ahh.' A feeling of waste took hold of her. She ought to be seeing this with someone. No longer consecrated to loneliness, she was impatient to reach her destiny.

She moved to the water's edge. Then she bent down and washed her hands and her wedding-ring – which was loose anyhow – began to slip off. She removed it, looked at it, put it to her lips, kissed it tenderly, and then threw it violently into the water. The last unwitnessed act of flinging her husband away. She stayed there for a while, not regretting it, lost in a patch of darkness, and then she decided to retire early so that she would look well the following day.

Chapter Seven

The violinist was located at the top of the building and next afternoon she set out for there. Along the quiet and empty corridor she walked, like a shadow, stealthily, and close to the wall. He had warned her not to be seen by guests. On the sixth landing she rested. He had warned her too about not taking the lift in case the lift operator might see her and watch where she went. By the time she got to his door she was out of breath. She tapped nervously and he opened it a little and drew her in. The first effect was of clutter and not much light. Musical instruments were strewn about and the feeling of constriction was terrible. It was an attic room, and compared with the majestic ballroom where he played each night, this was absurd.

His clothes were hung in an alcove and she saw the jacket that had first introduced her to him. Not sumptuous now but a best jacket carefully hung up so that it would be perfect for its evening's outing.

She said '*Bonjour*', but said it badly. All the way up the stairs she had practised saying it casually. He scratched idly at the hair on his chest, smiling at her, stretching his other arm to show the difference in their colouring. They were like people from different orbits. There was a smell of ozone from under his armpits. Then in his shorts, he stood before her and kissed her and positioned his legs so that they coincided with hers exactly. When she made a small change of position he moved his limbs too and she

thought, 'He's hurrying everything, he's rushing it.'
Over his bare, bronze shoulder she saw a camera on a
tripod, like an eye spying on her, and she drew back
quickly and asked what it was. She really meant, 'Why is
it there spying on me?'

'For photograph,' he said, and then remembering his
duties as a host he offered her apple juice.

'Have you whisky?' she said. She felt nervous. The
small room was suffocating and insects came in hordes
through the window space. He had taken the glass out
completely. She breathed out through her parted lips to
try and cool herself. The morning's heat had murdered
her. Sun got in the folds of her arms and legs, and she
gasped when she went out and saw the cars cooking on the
roadside and the brown bodies glistening with jelly and
not even a twilight under the trees where she ran to
escape.

'Spirits no gud,' he said handing her the half glass of
apple juice.

'Christ, I always pick the puritans,' she said, hoping he
would not know what she meant. He told her to sit on the
bed and then he got behind the camera and asked if he
could take a picture.

'I'm not very pretty,' she said, sitting all the same. She
saw him stoop down and heard something click and knew
that the picture when it was developed would show an
apprehensive woman, with a glass midway between her
chest and her open mouth. He crossed over and drew
down one strap of her dress so that it fell on her arm. The
white sagging top of one breast came into view. Above it
was a line of raw pink where she had boiled in the sun that
morning in an effort to get a tan for him. He photographed
her like that and then with both straps down so that the
sag of both breasts was in view and then he brought her
dress down around her waist and photographed her naked

top. It had been too hot to put on a brassière. From his position, stooped behind the camera, he indicated that she hold one breast, perkily, as if she enjoyed showing it off.

'I'm not well formed,' she said stupidly, and remembered, stupidly again, that breasts ought to be the shape of champagne glasses. Then she asked him to talk. Desire had snapped since the previous night, and she thought of elastic snapping and the ugly pimply look it got. She felt ugly like that.

'Take your dress . . .' and then he frowned. 'Your name?' he asked.

'Ellen,' she said, flatly.

'Ellen,' he said, and dwelt on it for a second, to please her. 'Ellen, take your dress right off, show the body,' he said. He pulled an imaginary dress down the length of his own body.

'I can't,' she said, her voice strangled with embarrassment.

'You are a holy woman,' he said.

'I am not a holy woman,' she said, although it would have been simpler to say yes.

'I want to talk,' she said. 'I want you to tell me about you and where you're from and who taught you the violin and why you do this.' She pointed to the camera and then looked for the other camera on the wash-stand. It was a small one with a treacherous little eye. Beside it a bundle of new towels in a Cellophane wrapping. On the Cellophane there was printed an English name. Her eye rested there, as if by looking at the English name she would escape the indignity happening to her.

'A gift,' he said, 'from Englishwoman.'

'Nice,' she said.

'They are nice,' he said. 'They are thought to be cold.' He repeated the word cold as if to confirm its meaning.

'You mean frigid,' she said, but he didn't seem to understand.

'The unmarried girls they only want cuddle, no business,' he said. 'No juice.'

'No juice,' she said, and asked about the English-woman who had sent him the gift. He said a nice lady she had been, and handsome. Ellen thought of some woman – bound to be in her thirties – going home to her husband with a guarded look, and having to keep the violinist's address in the toecap of her shoe and have the towels posted directly from the shop. Sadness began to wash over her, and thinking of lying in a sea of sadness she saw the waves as patient, painless and unceasing.

'You are from where?' she said, seriously trying to get on to another plane of friendship with him. He was from Vienna and had a flat separate from his parents. He had a sweetheart too, who sewed all her own dresses and looked smarter than any of the girls who spent fortunes in shops. He was engaged, and hoped to be married at the end of the summer, which was why he had to save and could not buy spirits for Englishwomen, not even nice English-women.

'And how would you feel if your sweetheart was un-faithful?' she said trying to stir his conscience so that he would make no scene when she drew her dress up.

'Sad,' he said. ' *Très, très* sad.' And she wished that she had never come and the jacket had been something she saw and stroked without knowing its owner.

'We not talk about such things, I think it a little beet un-natural,' he said.

'Un-natural,' she said, sitting there with the top of her dress bagging around her middle. She tried to hold her breasts up but the effort was extreme. Then she fanned herself with her silk purse and said,

'You and I will be special friends and not make love.'

'Oh yes, yes.' He rushed over.

If she resisted and screamed, would she be heard? Did other rapists occupy the attic rooms around? He drew her up by the hand and opened her zip, at snail's pace, and then looked at her in her half-slip. She stood there with the middle of her body death-white – a body that had never faced sunshine in its life – the ridiculous crescent of pink on her chest and two patches of pink on her thighs where the sun had hit them when she pulled her dress above her knees. He drew back the white cotton bed-spread and the one worn blanket underneath, and the top sheet. He rolled them back together and left the roll like a bolster at the end of the bed. Over the bottom sheet he spread a large bath towel. He did it thoroughly so that no inch of sheet was uncovered; she thought of the Englishwoman and why she sent him towels and she knew she could never lie down with him and make love.

'Come on,' he said, waiting for her to take off the frilled pants that she'd bought along with all the other honey-moon clothes.

He tried to help her with this and she knew that she had to say something to stop him.

'I think I'm going to bleed,' she said. The only thing that came to her lips.

'Bleed?' he said, not understanding.

'Blood,' she said, very clearly, and he frowned and said he did not like that very much.

'I do not like it very much either,' she said. He looked at her now with alarm, in case she might do the room an injury. He began to take the towel off the bed and fold it very carefully, first in two, then in four, then he put it on the towel rack near the wash-basin.

'I'm sorry,' she said.

'Too bat,' he said and suddenly he got very industrious

and took up a small notebook and asked her to spell the ugly word she had used. She wrote it down for him and thought if her husband ever needed evidence of her infidelity there was a half-naked, shivering picture of her on film and a word in her handwriting in his home-made phrase book. She said it was a verb and the infinitive was 'to bleed'.

'You are educated,' he said, surprised.

'I know about words,' she said, stepping into her dress, relieved, safe again.

'And this,' he asked, pointing to where her nipple lay, flat, under the flowered dress.

'Nipple.'

'Hot word,' he said. It took her a minute to understand that he wanted not ordinary words, but erotic ones for wooing Englishwomen.

'Just nipple,' she said.

'And you are a frigid woman,' he said, flicking the pages to F, where he could enter this new, unwelcome word. He was not as slow as she'd thought him to be. Then he lowered his hand between his legs and asked the juice words for there. He did not touch her any more, but kept looking suspiciously as if she were about to sully the place. When she sat down again – she did not feel nervous now – he rushed over with a plastic beach cushion and had her stand up so that he could put it under her.

'These region,' he said, pointing to her but not actually touching.

'Male or female?' she said, a little injured now.

'The both.'

'Well there's a vagina,' she said.

'Vagina no gud,' he said. He already knew that word. He wanted love words and pet words that would send Englishwomen rearing to the skies of abandon.

'Cunt, I suppose,' she said. He flicked the pages back

and wrote it under C. He wrote each word, carefully, in block letters.

'Though it can also be derogatory,' she said, 'if applied to a man.' He looked at her suspiciously as if she were making a fool of him.

'Cunt is all right for a woman,' she said.

'A woman is a cunt?' he said.

'A woman is a cunt,' she said. What did it matter if he ran into trouble. He deserved a few setbacks. She felt a fool, first for having come, then for having feigned bleeding, and now for not knowing a whole dictionary of love words so that he could stock up towels and other gifts for when he retired.

'May I have another drink?' she said, holding the glass out. He filled it quarter-ways and then began to busy himself about the room, picking up instruments, putting them down again, looking into his camera, looking through the window, frowning. She drank it down and left. He was putting on his shirt as she went out and he twiddled his fingers, but she could not see his face because it was lost in the vest. She would never forget the whites of his eyes.

Down in her bedroom she locked the door and sat straddled on the bidet, too fearful to wash herself. Because of the awful heat and what she'd told him she really felt that she might be bleeding. She could see nothing from her position on the bidet except one of the palms with the huge conical top. No matter where she went she saw one. They were beginning to be the only thing she noticed, the trees with the long trunks and their tops thrusting out from the sheath of whittled palms. She recalled everything they said, and thought if all the people in the world were as desperate as they then the world was a desperate place to be in. She sat for a long time but did not soap herself.

By dinner time she felt too despondent to go downstairs and ordered a meal to be sent up. The room-service boy wheeled the trolley in shortly after seven. He lifted the plate covers triumphantly as if he had been responsible for cooking the veal and dressing the salad and buttering the tiny little string beans.

'Mademoiselle, I fear I have mislaid my bus ticket,' he said, beaming at her.

'I fear I have too,' she said wryly. She sat quite still before the trolley and offered no resistance as he unfolded the cone of the napkin, shook it apart and then pressed it inside her shirt collar under her chin. She thought he petted her neck but could not be sure.

'*Bon*,' he said looking at the shirt. She had put on another stiff white shirt and a black silk skirt slit at one side. It seemed a waste to be eating in her room by herself, but she had dressed up simply to give herself some occupation.

'*Merci*,' she said, and waited with the knife and fork held in the air, above the plate, until such time as he went out.

Chapter Eight

She applied herself to her dinner. She gobbled everything together, tasting nothing, washing each mouthful down with the wine until her plate was suddenly and appallingly empty. It had taken seven minutes.

'Oh,' she said, as the door opened again and she leaped to her feet, thinking it was the chambermaid who had come to take off the outer bedspread. Her face was guilty from having eaten so fast.

'Listen,' she said then, the expression of guilt giving way to one of anger. It was him again. In plain clothes. Tight trousers. Open shirt. Wrist-watch. Hair on his arms.

'I fear I have mislaid my bus ticket,' he said, beaming because he knew the password, and delivered it so well. She took the tray, plonked it in his arms, and then walked towards the window, away from him. Foreign or not, he could not but perceive an insult like that. Behind her back she heard him open the door and place the tray outside, and then he said 'Look' very urgently as if disaster had struck. She turned towards him but saw that he was pointing to the window balcony and when she looked that way she saw that in the draught from the open door the pants hung there to dry had fallen down. Charged with shame she rushed across to pick them up and stuff them somewhere. When she stooped he came and put one hand on her breast and one lower down on her stomach. She straightened quickly and turned, but his face was upon hers in an attack of kissing. It took some seconds to realize what was happening.

As she rose he moved one hand to the butt of her back and helped her up and then laid her quickly on the bed. She thought ridiculously that if the chambermaid came in there would be a scandal, and through the onslaught of kisses she said, 'I don't want to do this,' but it was heard only as a mumble.

'How dare you,' she said then, clearly, getting her mouth free. She was angry with herself for ever having been so friendly. She thought that he must have seen something licentious in her smile or the offer of a cigarette earlier on, and then she wondered if he'd been in touch with the violinist and if the entire staff were not a network of vice passing on the names of the loose women.

She said, 'Control yourself,' three times. Long enough for her to free herself, stand up and put her hand to her hair in a gesture of composure.

'Five minutes,' he said, holding up five fingers.

'Five minutes,' she said, 'the entire population of women could be impregnated in five minutes if there were enough maniacs like you.'

He couldn't understand a word. He stood there with the five fingers held up, pleading. Even his hands repelled her. Up to then they had been hands doing work, toiling, buttering beans, bearing tea, but they had been planning other uses all along. Deceiver.

'I am a respectable woman,' she said calmly, and he tried to embrace her again.

'Look here,' she said, pushing him away, pointing to the telephone as a threat. He put his hands to his eyes and mimicked tears as if he were a small boy.

'You have the biggest cheek of anyone I ever met,' she said.

'*Désolé*,' he said in the crying voice.

She warned him that he would have to go, waited for a second and then opened the door wide. She held it like that until he went out and then with her back to the closed door she stood, taking short breaths, thinking of the shame of it, her eyes on that part of the counterpane which they'd ruffled. Quickly she began to smooth it.

'I've made two enemies,' she said, going back to the door. She felt something being put through the letter-box and thought it another English paper. Early that morning a paper had thudded through and she read about the country she had come away to forget. Without turning she put her hand down and started, not knowing what the soft thing was. A flower. A red carnation. Not exactly fresh. Not withered either. She took it in and let the letter-box snap. The stem dripped in her hand. Straight from the hotel vase he'd taken it. He had nice instincts. And was ashamed of himself. She held it and smelt it, pouching its face the way he had pouched hers and she thought how foolish he'd been and she was not angry any more. At least the incident had livened her up. She was ready to go out now and wondered where to. She'd change again.

Half in and half out of the orange button-through dress she saw her door being abruptly opened for the second time that evening.

'God almighty,' she said as he came in with a plate bearing two apples and an ivory-handled peeling knife. He brought the plate towards her, offering it, like an apology. If it had been one apple she might have accepted.

'You're going too far,' she said as she finished buttoning her dress, then picking up her handbag she walked out of the room and left him standing in the middle of the floor with the peace offering at arm's length.

She went to the bathroom to repair her face, then walked down the two flights of wide, carpeted stairs and across the main hall to the lounge where she ordered a

Bloody Mary to steady her nerves. The bar was empty as most people were at dinner. From the dining-room came the clatter of dishes lost in the murmur of talk, and behind the talk the thin syrup music of a violin.

'*Merci*,' she said when the man brought the drink and the dish of almonds. She sampled it and licked the red juice from her upper lip and wished that she were meeting the violinist for the first time and that he were a different sort of person. The lights were in the trees as they had been the previous night, except that this time she noticed the cable wire running up along the trunks and the lights did not seem so magical any more. Before each sip of drink she took an almond and chewed it slowly and then she drank slowly, holding each mouthful and tasting it fully. There was all the time in the world.

'Isn't it great, great,' the only other person in the room said as she wriggled her shoulders and then stretched the upper half of her body to suit the drawn-out chord of music. Her torso was long and fluid and she wore a flowered dress of green silk that seemed to cling without being tight. She moved freely inside the dress and her movements were effective. Ellen pretended to listen to the quieter music. There were two sounds, one very loud from the barman's radio and the orchestra music farther away. She and the girl were the only people drinking and they looked a little unreal and diminutive in the big mirrored room with chandeliers above them and the empty wicker chairs and the empty circular tables repeated over and over again because of the many mirrors.

'Don't you love it,' the other girl said, snapping her fingers and letting her head loll from side to side. Although she flirted with the barman she kept looking towards the arch that led to the dining-room as if she expected someone to come through. The barman put the radio right up on the high counter and indicated that she should dance.

'I'm wild,' she said, and turning to Ellen finished the sentence, 'about that tune.'

'It's nice,' Ellen said.

'It's great,' the girl said. Her voice was purposely low and she stretched each word as if by stretching she would put emphasis into them. She was American. Her face was thick and sensual and not at all like her body, and her lips were thick too and fruity, stained with a lipstick the colour of blackberry juice. She wore no jewellery except a charm bracelet, and now and then she raised her wrist and shook it so that all the little charms fell in the same direction. They were like medals really.

'Are you here long?' Ellen said, wondering if this was another face which looked different down on the beach.

'I gotten here late this afternoon, and who is the first person I meet in the elevator and he thought he knew me!' She mentioned a well-known movie actor and said he was having dinner at that moment.

'Thought he knew me,' she said again. 'And he did the wildest thing. He beat his chest and he said, "Me a cowboy, me a cowboy, me a Mexican cowboy."' She laughed and clicked to the barman to bring two more drinks. Ellen had already put the note down to pay for hers. She felt reluctant about taking drink from a stranger.

'I'm fine,' she said.

'No, you're not,' the girl said and repeated the order for two more Bloody Marys. She came and sat at Ellen's table but looked towards the dining-room and did not even respond when the barman brought the two new drinks, more nuts and her bill. He also brought Ellen's change from the previous drink.

'I stopped off in Paris to get some pants, and then made right for this place,' she said, pushing one arm ahead of her to show her drive. The charms on the bracelet rattled when she did that.

'No, you have them, baby,' she said pushing the plate of nuts back to Ellen. She spanned her waist then and said, 'Not that I think food is fattening, I think it's all to do with your metabolism.' But Ellen had heard that from other women and knew that it was a dodge to make everyone but themselves gross.

'Do you like olives?' she said. Ellen said yes and set the two francs she'd been given as change on a race, like bicycle wheels across the table. One dropped off the edge and the barman rushed over to pick it up for her. She took it from him and started a new race and said very idly to her friend, who was called Denise, 'After the rich, the most obnoxious people in the world are those who serve the rich.'

'Boy, you've got problems,' Denise said, then stopped short because an exodus of people came through the arch. Hitching her dress up she lay back in the chair and stretched her legs full length. With the mirrors it was unlikely that she could be missed.

'Here they come,' she said in a whisper and then in her low, calculating drawl she spoke, 'I just love olives, I went right across America once and I lived on three things, beer, avocado pears and olives. Right across the country. I ended up in a little town called – I forget what 'twas called but you have no idea how beautiful our country is.' It was well and professionally timed and he halted under one of the chandeliers and did the 'Me a cowboy' again, beating his chest over-humbly. He was with a large group, the men stood when he stood and older women filed behind, linking and talking earnestly. There were a few young girls walking straight with their stomachs held in. Ellen registered no face except his. She'd never seen him in the films, but he had a striking presence. He had the look of the gutter about him. She thought of men in lorries who whistle at girls' legs and have bare dolls as mascots on their windshields. He was common and wild and undeniably handsome.

'How about asking them to join us for a drink?' one of the men said, and Denise let out a gurgle of shock as if an electric current had been passed through her. Ellen went on racing her coins, but careful now to put a hand at the other edge of the table to save them from falling off.

'Girls, pretty girls,' one of the older women said. She had a fur stole on with tassels of fur at the end of it, which made the stole itself look silly.

'It so happens we would like to ask you ladies for a drink,' the actor said, loudly. Ellen and Denise looked at each other, hesitated and then Denise said, 'It's very funny that you should ask us because we're actually having a drink.' She had moved forwards, though, in her chair.

'Hey . . .' he said.

'Hey yourself,' she said and got up. Ellen rose almost immediately. The first thing she ought to make clear was that they weren't sisters, they weren't even friends.

'We just struck up a conversation,' she said.

'Tell me,' said an older man guiding her politely towards the door, 'have I seen you somewhere before?'

'Not that I know of,' she said, looking at him. His face was yellow from the heat and his eyes were light blue and he must have been handsome once upon a time. His name was Sidney.

Within minutes they were in cars swooping down the drive towards the main part of the town where the activity was. Ellen sat in the back of a chauffeur-driven Bentley between Sidney and the woman with the fur-tipped stole. The tips brushing her legs had the stealth of an animal sneaking up on her and she wondered how much it had cost. The movie actor was in front, talking to Denise about muscle. He believed in fights.

'I don't know anyone's name,' Ellen said to the two people she sat between.

'She doesn't know anyone's name,' said the woman who called herself Gwynnie. 'Isn't that cute?'

'That's terrible,' the actor said in a false voice of sympathy, and turning he patted her knee and said, 'Do me a favour, call me Bobby.' She was a little embarrassed and did not know what to say.

'Go on,' he said.

'Bobby,' she said. Then he smiled and said she had the sort of voice he could listen to all night and he did not seem insulting at all.

'Stick around,' he said, giving her a friendly pat and then putting Gwyn's fur stole back on her bare knees. There was not only luxury but security in being covered by the fur. She thought perhaps this response was first caused by having seen a couple make love within a belted beaver coat, in an alleyway, in childhood, years before. They'd shooed her away as if she were a dog, when in fact she'd wanted not to spy but to behold.

They converged on a night-club that was so dimly lit that it was like going into a cinema. The manager welcomed Sidney, and three tables were put together for them and a pile of chairs brought. They sat wherever they happened to have been standing. She was between Sidney and another man who told her he was Bobby's understudy. Opposite was Bobby, Denise, and a pretty boy with a less pretty boy, joined to each other by two gold bracelets that were clipped together with a little gold padlock. She tried to smile at them but they were very aloof. There were about twenty people in all: a wide-shouldered man called Jason, whose wife had the fur-tipped stole, and some oriental girls with slit skirts, who never spoke, and the older women chirping like birds, and a platoon of people who said, 'Isn't that marvellous?'

whenever the actor, Sidney, or Jason, the powerful element of the group, opened their mouths.

'I definitely dig her, she is a law unto herself,' the man Jason kept saying of some woman who lived on the East coast of America and wrote for movies.

'How do you mean?' Sidney said.

'I mean she's a law unto herself,' Jason said, and his wife told the group that this girl came to stay with them one week-end when the temperature was in the nineties and wore pretty blouses all the time with sleeves that came right down to the wrist, and then she discovered the girl having a shower in the bathroom and found that she had this big growth on her arm with hair on it. The story sent a shiver through the gathering and Bobby said for God's sake to get the drinks before they all went to sleep or something. At the word sleep Denise put her head on his shoulder and basked there for a second.

'Don't forget we've a date, I'm twenty-five at midnight,' she said, pretending to be drunker than she was.

'All rightie,' Gwyn said as the waiter came with the first bucket of champagne. Vapour clouded the bucket except where his fingers had touched it, in putting it down, and there, four squat prints showed shiny. He brought four other tubs and various squat bottles of whisky with the black-and-white label she knew well, and fruit juice for the slim oriental girls.

'You're having what?' Sidney asked as he dealt out numerous packets of cigarettes like a pack of cards. He was proud to be host to so many people and was paying particular attention to Ellen.

'I'd like Pernod,' she said, and Bobby who was half-way through a tumbler of whisky put it down and said he'd like that too.

'What would I do without you?' he said, smiling over at her. She smiled back. He said they must look at etchings some time. The evening was beginning to bloom.

'Bobby's the best in the world, the best in the world,' the understudy kept telling her. She couldn't see how he would fill in if Bobby fell sick. He had thicker features and spoke with oily Irish-American gusto, whereas Bobby had a sharp-boned face and spoke in a low, lazy manner.

'Gave me forty-seven suits, no kiddin',' he said. 'And my son got married and on their wedding day they didn't know it but they had a honeymoon paid for, in Bermuda.'

'Did they go?' she said, thinking, 'Supposing they didn't want to go?'

'Did they go!' he said, affronted. 'They had the time of their lives. Never forget it. Forty-seven suits he gave me, no kiddin'.'

'Why don't you kill him?' she said, 'then you could afford to buy your own suits.' She hated his humbleness, his tell-you-the-honest-truth, jarvey driver's drivel.

'Hemlock,' she said. 'I have it on good authority, boil the roots.'

'I was married to a woman like you once,' he said, his face ground into a temper.

'And you killed her,' she said quickly.

He got up and took his drink and dragged his chair to the end of the table. She pretended not to notice and looked around as if she were looking for someone special. A little boy on a woman's lap sat with his mouth open, his face enraptured by the noise, the lights and the great, green, spreading tree that was the roof. She missed her son then and thought of the resonance of all their kissing and wished that she could hold him in her arms. She shut her eyes and tried to memorize the shape of his face, but it eluded her. She searched for it frantically, in her mind, through shut eyes.

'Wake up, ma'am, we're going to have a ball,' Bobby said. Their drinks had come. The waiter brought the

Pernod as he had been told to: an ice filter laid into each tall glass with small chinks as tiny and as splintered as diamonds, and a jug of water. Bobby did the pouring and as the water seeped through the filter the harsh green Pernod began to cloud, and looking from one green to another, she saw his eyes like the whey of the milk, and above them the great, green, spreading tree. She looked up at the tree, still trying to recall her son's face, and he looked too, and was softened by the sight of it, and raising his glass he said:

'Marje.'

'I'm not Marje,' she said.

'I know you're not Marje,' he said, 'but cheers,' and still looking at the tree he asked if she had ever heard of white peaches.

'Are there white peaches?' she asked, shaking her head with surprise, with pleasure.

'You can say that again.' He described how they grew in New England and with his hands suggested how they squelched as they touched the ground. Because of a fatal softness.

'I would love to see one,' she said, not meaning that, but meaning, 'You are nicer and less tough than you look.'

'I like you,' she said then.

'I knew you would,' he said. 'I can read thoughts.' It was beginning to be an adventure. The drink warmed her. A small boy in sequins was announcing the most fabulous strip tease of the season. Sidney said they could both watch and carry on their conversation. They had been discussing an American novelist.

'He's not a nigger writing about niggers, he's a fairy writing about fairies,' Sidney repeated, proud of his assessment.

'Don't talk like that,' Gwyn said, injured, and looked towards the homosexuals as if they'd been hurt. They

64

were absorbed in each other, and testing who could touch the farthest point of his nose with his tongue. The younger boy had a very clear and very pointed tongue, which he brandished like a knife. He could touch his nose quite easily with it, but his lover who was older found difficulty in doing the trick. Afterwards the older one gulped as if the exercise had made him sick. They seemed quite happy in their relationship.

'He's writing about fairy niggers, that's what he's doing,' Bobby said suddenly. He had a knack of picking up the thread wherever the talk seemed liveliest.

'Big theme!' Jason said in his powerful voice.

'You see that stole, Jason, well that's the one I always wanted,' Gwyn said as she pointed to a woman who wore a cape of dark mahogany-coloured fur. It was the darkest, furriest fur Ellen had ever seen. You expected it to creep, it was so like an animal.

'You never said, honey,' he replied, patting his wife as if she were some sort of patient. Then he said to the actor, 'He's not even a nigger, for God's sake,' and an elderly lady from the next table requested to get the Yanks out. Her hair which was blonde was in a plait and she waved this menacingly at them. Then the lights were switched off completely and in the darkness Ellen heard Denise say to the actor:

'How 'bout us doing the shakes out of here?' He didn't move. On stage a woman on tip-toe circled a double bed which had a very frilly coverlet. Bathed in mauve spot-light the woman started to undress. She wore black mesh stockings and heels so high that she looked like some sort of bird perched on long, thin legs. As she disrobed she threw each garment to the audience. The actor caught her third and innermost petticoat, smelt it, and said, 'A nursing mother,' loud enough for everyone to hear.

There was laughing from various tables and a fan said

his name affectionately. Sidney was pleased. When the girl was naked except for the petals over her breasts and the kerchief lower down, she took a natural-colour fox fur and began to draw it back and forth, slowly between her legs. Each time she moved it she let out a moan and a muscle in her bare thighs quivered. She had taken off her stockings too. There were whistles and gasps from the various tables. The first orgasm of the evening.

'I can't stand it, I tell you I can't stand it,' Gwyn said. She was sobbing. Jason took an enormous handkerchief and held it over her eyes, and she sobbed and kept saying it was an insult.

'You hold it,' he said. Ellen looked from the woman sobbing to the dancer teasing the audience and then in matchlight at hordes of ants advancing over the table-cloth, and suddenly her son's face came to her: in his duffle coat with the hood framing his round pale face, emphasizing his big eyes. She thought of the holiday he and his father were having; the pure unsullied days: digging for worms in the morning, fishing the rivers when the sun went down, slitting a trout open on the river bank and taking the insides out, tipping them back in the river; the smell of methylated and wood smoke; he would make a second fire to keep the flies off, and eating the trout off the new tin plates they would dip their bread in the frying-pan to get the last of the lovely black, savoury, melted butter. She licked her lips for them. The lights on the top half of the dancer were lurid now and dark down below. The natural-colour fox was black between the legs. You could hear a pin drop. Everybody except the actor was engrossed. She caught his eye and he leaned across and said something to her.

'A what?' she said.

'It's a man,' he said and she asked how.

'It's behind,' he said, pressing his thumb on to his palm

and hiding it there to show that the man had likewise hidden part of himself. Then the music got very fast and the dancer discarded the fox tail and hung the rubber breasts on either bed post and stood naked except for a triangle of black sequins above the thighs. It was a man who had perfectly mimicked all the coquette of a woman. People clapped, but some must have felt cheated as Ellen did. She also felt a little sick.

'You're all right?' Sidney asked.

'I'm hungry,' she said. She was ashamed to say that she felt disgusted. Gwyn was blowing her nose now into the big handkerchief. It was navy with white spots. It could have been a scarf really. The oriental girls smiled as if they'd just seen a religious ceremony.

'Hungry,' the actor said. He ordered some artichokes because it was too late to get real food.

'Oh, baby, don't be silly,' Denise said to her, drunk now and not caring what she said.

'I can't eat artichokes,' Ellen said appealing to the actor. On stage a boy was singing *Anyone who had a heart*, and the English were joining in because it was the craze song in England at that time. She thought of Hugh Whistler and for the first time had no regrets about his going away. His indifference had fated her to this gathering and this gathering was exotic in a way that no Englishman could ever be.

'You're going to learn.' Bobby came and sat next to her. Two artichokes were brought and a small dish of very yellow mayonnaise.

'Not enough here for a midget,' he said, picking one of the outer leaves, dipping its base in the mayonnaise and then nudging her to watch. With his top teeth he grazed the white base that was covered over with the mayonnaise.

'Good,' he said. 'It's a good artichoke.' Sucking it

meditatively he said it was going to get better the deeper they got in. He enjoyed showing her.

'Try it,' he said. She picked a leaf and watched what he did and then did the same thing. They ate slowly at first and then they began to race it and the leaves got purpler as they went deeper but the white parts were just the same. They put the grazed leaves in front of them on the table and she was doing almost as well as he was.

'Oh,' she said, surprised by the sheath of hairs that covered the heart. She had no idea it was going to be like that. She thought of the fox tail again but felt happier now.

'I love it,' he said. 'It's like a woman.' They were very close and secretive, and she watched, ignoring the singing all round them as he made incisions with the sharp end of his penknife, nicking the hairs all round the base of the heart.

'They get in the back of your neck and you know it,' he said as she watched and held her breath while he slit the cap of hair right off and exposed the grey-white heart underneath. She felt as if he had been doing it to her.

'Ma'am,' he said, pushing the plate in front of her.

'But it's yours,' she said, remembering how he said it was like a woman.

'You have it,' he said, 'and I'll whip you later.' He watched while she tasted it. It may have been the ritual attached, or his company, or the three drinks, but it seemed to be the most subtle thing she had ever tasted.

'I love anything that is trouble to get,' she said, chewing, pretending to like it even more than she did, although the flavour was good and it had a strange texture.

'I know you do,' he said as he prepared the second one for her. She could see a man looking at her from another table. He wore dark glasses and had dark bushy hair. When he caught her eye he lowered the glasses a little on to his nose and beamed at her. The room-service boy. She burst out laughing. He thought it an invitation and stood up to come over.

'The room-boy from the hotel,' she said to Bobby, 'is following me around.'

'So?' he said.

'He raped me this evening,' she said, wanting to make a story out of it now.

'How was it?' He could be aloof and sarcastic quicker than anyone she ever met.

'Not as good as this,' she said, biting into the second heart.

'Front or back?'

'Side,' she said, wanting to be as bright and brittle as all the other people. Some of the party were standing and some were objecting about having to go and Denise kept saying, 'I'm damned if I'm going to be twenty-five in this position,' and Bobby said to bring it with her and she went out chewing the last of the artichoke. The room-boy positioned himself near the door but she pretended not to see him. Mosquitoes like particles of dust were moving around the outside lights and people were walking around as if it were the middle of the day.

'Same cars as last time,' Sidney said.

'Where are we going?' Ellen asked Bobby, linking them both so that she could raise herself off the ground, just the way her son did when he was happy.

'How are you doing?' Bobby said.

'She's doing fine,' Sidney said. 'Like an eight-year-old.' She was as breathless and as buoyant as she ever remembered having been. Happiness was surely pending.

Chapter Nine

They drove out of the town and along by the coast, through Cannes. Someone pointed out a tall hotel with a white decorative front and it reminded her of tier upon tier of wedding cake. Then they took a narrow road and began to climb. It was hot. All the windows were down. Now and then at bends in the road she felt that an on-coming car had just shaved them and she was vaguely nervous but not frightened enough to protest. The driver had been drinking with them. Through the open window she watched the clouds slip between her and the moon and thought, This is living at last. A little drunk. Sidney's arm around her neck. Bobby, though he was in front, took the trouble to stretch his elbow back and rest it on her knee. Reassurance. And an instant of danger from an-other passing car. The narrow steep road, the gears constantly grinding, the climb, the moon through the window and the fields twined with vines running down to meet the road. Sometimes there were walls and some-times not.

'How are you doing?' Bobby often said, turning round. He was in front with Denise.

'Give my love to the pilchards,' Ellen said. Up to then she had struggled to keep sober, but now she thought they were all behaving a little drunk and silliness was appro-priate. She thought Denise said 'Crap', but could not be sure.

'Here's to sex,' Gwyn was saying. Someone had brought

a bottle of whisky and it was being passed round. The driver refused it. Ellen said she wanted to have it after Bobby, to have a taste of him. They all laughed.

'There's my girl,' he said.

'Sex within marriage,' Gwyn said.

'If I were six months younger,' Sidney said, his arm tightening round Ellen's neck, until she felt she'd choke, 'we'd get married . . .' and then the car was brought to a sudden grinding halt and the screech of the brakes was more desperate than the 'Sweet Jesus', that Gwyn let out. It was on a very deserted part of the road with no houses around. As soon as they stopped the cars behind had to stop too and there was an outrage of hooting.

'General de Gaulle kidnapped,' Bobby said and made a joke about having to build a private oratory for him to hear Mass every day.

'And a mermaid on Fridays,' Denise said, and then Gwyn said they ought to be ashamed of themselves ridiculing Catholics like that. They waited for a few minutes with the engine running, and cars hooting from behind, and the men making middling jokes, when the driver got out. When he came back he appeared to be trembling. A motor-cyclist was dead a few yards up.

'Really dead?' Ellen said, as if there was still a chance to prevent it.

'Looks so,' the driver said, and Gwyn said they ought to get a priest or something. They all got out. A small group of people surrounded the spot where the accident had happened. Their faces looked stricken and they had their eyes down because of the blinding headlights from a police car. They stood solemnly and watched as they would never have watched if this man had been alive. The actor pushed his way through. Over his shoulder Ellen saw the body, thrown forward from the motor-cycle which was in the centre of the road. A black car with wings like a giant bird was sprawled across the road where it had obviously swerved to avoid him. His trousers appeared to be empty of his legs and one boot was a few yards away. His sock was running blood.

'He was doing eighty,' a voice said. Most people talked in French. Someone said he was German. His papers were German. She shivered at the thought of falling ill or dying in a strange country. She wanted to go home, not to London to the pipes of light but home to the race to which she belonged: and then she shivered uncontrollably, knowing that their thoughts were no longer hers. She had vanished back into childhood and the dark springs of her terrors. She quickly memorized prayers, saw bog-holes into which animals stupidly plunged, and a mountain lake where two mad women drowned themselves. No houses for miles around. The lake itself lyric and deceptive on a summer's day. With water-lilies on its gentle surface. More leaf than flower. She dreaded death. She thought of a young priest who came to warn her once when she started to wade out to sea at a point where bathing was dangerous. His eyes brimmed over with soft love. He'd asked nervously if she'd seen the sign. She hadn't. She could have died but for him, unprepared, shocked and unwilling. She thanked him with her own eyes and wanted to touch his pale hands and move her fingers towards his wrists, lost in big black cassock sleeves. But she did not dare in case of encroaching on his chastity. She reached out and gripped Bobby's bare arm and clung to him the way she had wanted to cling to the priest with the soft eyes and the austere, Christ-like, disciplined hands.

'Looking at it does no good,' she said to Bobby. He didn't hear because he and Jason were trying to restrain Gwyn.

'Listen, baby, it's none of your business,' Jason said as

he caught her by the stole. She detached herself and one end of the stole trailed along the road in the dust. Eventually it would be touched by the dead man's blood, which was making small courses in different directions.

'As a Catholic, it's my duty,' she said. She was trying to get to the dead man to say an Act of Perfect Contrition in his ear.

'*Attention!*' a policeman said, blocking her way. A second policeman had a notebook out and was taking statements in French. In the ghostly light, part moon, part headlights, everyone looked guilty. He was deader than anyone Ellen had ever seen. She did not dare look on his face. Then the ambulance came and they got the stretchers out and police asked those who had not witnessed the accident to return to their cars. They got in the car and she was in front this time. Being third in line they got away quickly. Quite a queue of cars had gathered up behind.

'Well what about the war, what about it?' Jason kept saying as his wife accused him of having no feeling.

'I always knew you were hard, always,' she kept saying.

'Should make us all think a little deeper,' Jason said then as if he were making a speech.

'Poor bastard,' Bobby said.

'He died on his face,' Gwyn said suddenly and with animosity.

'He was on his back,' Ellen said, and looked to the others for confirmation.

'Listen, my girl, we picked you up and brought you out of that dump tonight, otherwise you'd have gotten nowhere,' Gwyn said and one of the men said to shut up, that a man was dead.

'We know he's dead, nobody's saying he's not dead,' Jason said, and they were all a little on edge and sober now. The driver was taking it easy too. Ellen kept looking out of the window. There were no landmarks except signs advertising night-clubs, and road danger-signals, and high walls around houses. Sometimes there was no wall and it felt dangerous then. The fields when she could see them were very steep and tilled. Each row of tillage was buttressed by a row of stone. The stone kept the soil from being washed down the steep hills in heavy rain. She wanted to be like that, supported, by a solid man. Her husband would be asleep now, under stars, with frogs and other night animals moving about in the hay field outside. He was a strong man whom she'd thrown away, not for a year, not for an age, but for ever. She was afraid she might cry, so she started to hum blithely: 'Anyone who had a heart.' Someone said she was callous.

When they got to Sidney's house the other two cars were already there. They'd got off the main road, they said, after they saw the hold-up of cars.

'Was that boy lying on his face or not?' Gwyn asked one of the oriental girls. The girl just looked at her and said nothing. Ellen hurried in the house in case there might be a scene. She entered a huge hallway with tapestries on the wall and a big table covered from end to end with sunhats. There were hats with their crowns laid into other hats and some piled on each other, their straw canes sticking up like haystalks. There must have been hundreds of hats in all. Suddenly she wished that she had not come. The evening had turned sour after what they'd seen. People climbed the marble stairs in silence. Only the homosexuals seemed close but that may have been because they were manacled together.

'You saw it?' she said, first to one, then to the other.

'*Oui*,' they said as calmly as if they had seen a leaf drop from a tree.

'I think I ought to go home,' she said, turning to Sidney who was on the bottom step directing people up.

'I wouldn't hear of it,' he said.

'Chrissake relax, we haven't beaten you yet,' Bobby said. She went on climbing but was not happy about it, any more.

Chapter Ten

'Listen Fellas we don't have to turn it into a wake,' Jason said when they were all in. Some of the men said, 'Quite right,' and Sidney said a drink wouldn't be a bad idea. When he rang, white-coated waiters came in from the shadows of the hall. The elder women grouped together comparing what they had seen of the accident and one of the oriental girls sat on a chair that tipped back when she sat, so that she appeared to be floating. Her long brown legs stretched out in front of her. The homosexuals took down a book of illustrations that they'd obviously been engrossed in before they went out because there was a fairly fresh blue delphinium as a bookmark. They were coloured drawings of diseased parts of the human body. She saw a warty breast discharging pus and looked to see their responses. Their faces were quite calm and they took turns in moving the pages. Their prisoned hands were out of sight under the table. She moved away and hid her bag behind a chair – a habit from her young days when she went to dance halls in Ireland and hid the purse that contained her cloakroom ticket, her rosary beads and perhaps a shilling.

'It's beautiful,' she said to Sidney as he stood there waiting for her to say something about his house. It was an enormous room, a garden really, with the heavens as a roof and for walls a serration of trees that stooped harmoniously towards the sea several hundred feet below. Lights nesting in the trees were softened by the lantern of leaves and there were mirrors in the loops of branches to multiply those lights. Wooden and stone busts rose like ogres out of some trees and in the spacious darkness everyone seemed enhanced. So different from the place they'd left. The long refectory table was being laid at that hour.

'Make yourself at home,' Sidney said.

'Thank you,' she said.

She looked around for Bobby. He was describing a scene to an elderly woman. It was obviously a scene where he came in and was shot in the belly straight away because he was staggering as he acted it. The woman, who had white cotton hair and an old rouged face, looked as if she was being made love to. And he was smiling. Soft and lovely now with the green forest light upon him.

'Taste this,' Sidney said as her eyes wandered.

She sipped a colourless liquor that was made from coconut. Sweet on her tongue, it quickly turned to fire as it caught her throat.

She gasped, smiled, took another sip and gasped again.

'In Russia,' she said, 'there is a verb, created for what I am doing, a special verb for the special sigh . . .'

'You're full of shit,' Denise said, overhearing the latter half of the sentence.

'My lungs are on fire,' Ellen said to Sidney, ignoring Denise. Sidney said he was already six months younger and drew her across to the table so that they could inspect the food which had just been brought.

'Isn't that precious?'

'And look at the butter, he's crazy, that cook.'

A mound of butter had been patted into the shape of the house, with a wide door, big downstairs windows and turret windows along the top. Sidney was very pleased.

'He's a good boy, Antonio,' he said then, and someone said wasn't it true that no matter how late Sidney stayed out Antonio waited at the hall door to receive him.

'Slavery,' Ellen said under her breath. The story was both sad and loving. She remembered then that a middle-aged man in a white coat had been at the door when they drove up. He was standing there rubbing his hands together, but he disappeared as they got out.

'Eat, eat,' Sidney said, touching her elbow. She moved away.

There was a vast choice. Thick red soup had been brought in individual dishes, with blobs of sour cream on some. There was an enormous salmon, its skin the bright silver it must have been when hauled out of a river in Scotland, and the peaches were peeled of their cloth-like skins and purposely bruised so that the kirsch could soak through them. She loved the smell of kirsch and bent down to inhale it with both nostrils. She had soup first. It was thick as jelly and thrillingly cold. The look of the salmon disturbed her. She thought of them again, rivers, damp soil, hanging their wet socks on a branch to dry, the tent in a shady place, the special lyric purity of everything he did, even of the type of holiday he chose for the child.

'Have a peach,' Bobby said as he came across and searched her face for the cause of its sudden despondency.

'I want you to send me one of your white peaches,' she said, sucking a yellow one out of his hand. He had a spoonful of the kirsch too which he brought to her lips and coaxed her to drink, like a mother offering medicine to a favourite child.

'They don't travel, ma'am,' he said and paused, his eyes roaming over her face. 'But I'll take you there, how about that?'

'To an orchard,' she said, hanging on his promise.

'Don't be greedy,' he said, but in a nice way as he began to describe the place in New England where the peaches grew. She could see them, large and fleshy-white and hear the squelch they made in the ear as you pressed them. But she was thinking really of little white berries that grew along hedges in Ireland, with which they used to frighten each other at school, by suddenly bursting them in some unsuspecting ear. He brought her inside his world, with his low voice, and his habit of saying 'Ma'am', and his face and his thin, hard, electric body that never rested. He had been all over. Rocky Mountains. Peru. Mexico. And in fights. He worked on a chain gang at sixteen. Drunk weeks. Sober weeks. And had muscle.

'Feel that,' he said as she touched the top of his arm and felt the caged strength and said, 'Iron,' looking into the green of his eyes and thinking again that they had the light, lucid green of the whey of the milk. The muscle seemed to grow in her grasp. He was sweet and childish. All that and white peaches.

'Fall backwards,' he said when she let go of his arm.

'I can't,' she said, 'I have no co-ordination.'

'Damn right you haven't,' he said, 'but I'll teach you.'

Then he spread his hand out and the quickness and deftness of that spread was like an eagle opening its wings, although she knew about eagles only from hearsay. He had the fingers apart, roughly the same distance between each one and the palm slightly hollowed to receive her fall.

'Come on,' he said, and with the other hand pushed her back a little, but when she sloped back she was like a rod that would not bend.

'Trust me,' he said, gently now so that she forgot the tough talk and the fights and drunk weeks. She fell but not naturally and he said, 'Great,' to give her encouragement for the next fall. He stood behind her, moving a little farther away at each new fall so that she was taking greater and greater risks. They did not say a word. Each time he caught her surely and beautifully and she loved the certainty of his hand and would stay like that for longer than was necessary, half-way towards the floor, her weight resting on him. And never once did he squeeze her neck or flirt with her but she knew he was making love to her all the same.

In her lovely girl's phase now she smiled slyly and made assignation with him and thought, 'I have white thighs, long arms, a face, teeth, knees, hip bones, a curving belly and the tuft of silken hair that all men want to comb through, and I won't let anyone else take him for this night's pleasure,' and she said, 'I want to tell you a story.'

'I wish you would,' he said and linking her now he drew her over to the balustrade that faced the tropical garden as it ran down to the sea. She thought frantically of what story might amuse him, and tipping the last of the kirsch from the saucer fed it to him from the spoon and put her foot on his instep curling her toes around his, unfolding a story:

'It is a long-legged bird in Ireland that lives alone near a lake. It eats raw fish all the time and shits it out straight away and sometimes gets so tired of eating and shitting and shitting and eating that it puts its behind on a stone and stays there to let the stone hold the fish in. A fisherman watched it for hours sitting on the stone and the minute it stood up . . .'

He laughed quickly and said what a fine girl he'd met and they were really laughing and really happy.

'It's over here, it's all happening over here,' Denise said behind them.

'Come on now, none of this sneaky laughing.' Jason came between them and parted them with a breast stroke.

'God that's funny,' Bobby said and told everyone how funny it was and she had to tell it again except that it was not funny the second time and when she'd finished she said, 'It's just a little . . . story,' and drew away.

Sidney followed her into the garden, down the steep

steps towards the sea. So many steps it was dizzying. She couldn't descend naturally. She kept using the same foot – the right one – all the time the way she did in a cinema if she came in and the picture was on.

'Take your shoes off,' he said, 'and I'll carry them.' He carried them by their sling-back straps. Gold they were and like little lamps in his hand, hanging down.

'It was a nice story,' he said.

'I've never walked barefoot before,' she said, truly surprised that the pine needles were needly.

'They should be carpet-soft,' she said.

'No,' he said, 'they should not,' and they both thought of a song about 'Where is the chicken that has no bone', and they hummed it lightly, to themselves, but for each other, as they went down the steps towards the sea, purposeful.

He brushed the marble seat with his handkerchief before she sat and sitting she found it cold and sobering and imagined it would be like that to sit on a glacier. By now she had reconciled herself to the fact that he would want to kiss her, but she did not mind that because she knew that Bobby was there and the night would not be desolate. All her outings and hopes were veered towards being with a certain kind of man that controlled and bewitched her. Bobby was such a man.

The sea was busy, the waves moving in a frantic way as if mirrors were held creating mad disturbances.

'What does the sea remind you of?' she asked, in order to postpone the kiss.

'Nothing, just itself. What about you?'

'Thoughts,' she said, and hoped it did not sound pretentious, because it was true. Thoughts batting in and out of her head. She had seen no birds and no bats since she came.

'Like what?' he said. He had trained himself to listen.

'Oh everything,' she said, wishing she had never started on it. She could see her son's face now with blackcurrant jam all over his mouth and his eyes liquefying at the prospect of a new pot of jam.

'Tell me some of them,' he said, 'I'm really a dull chap.'

'We're all that,' she said. She wanted to grow grey and decline under his eyes so that he would not ask for anything.

'You're not dull,' he said. 'You have the strength of aeons.'

'Is that a quote?' she said.

'I'm sure it is, everything I say is a quote; even when I say movies are better than ever . . .'

'Tell you a nicer quote,' she said, placing her hand prayer-wise over his, 'It's about a bird, and it says, "Oh beautiful bird you fly so well no one would know you have but one wing, and you will never make the forest."'

'Wait a minute,' he said, 'I must catch up. Single syllables for years,' and he then mimicked his own voice, saying, 'No,' and 'No, no, listen, Charlie, I wouldn't spring a deal like that on you . . . You know me, Charlie.'

She thought of his money and wondered how great the sacrifice had been and how many people he had killed along the way. Yellow all around, the lemons in the trees like lobes of light, the odd lit bulb, and his face yellow like parchment, from age. His blue eyes were not dead but were something worse. They had the sick look of eyes that were wounded and for whom death would be a relief. Did he look at the illustrations too and reflect upon disease, taking pleasure in it as only the maimed can? Except that he was so sad.

'You wanted to kiss me,' she said. 'Well you can do it now.' And she closed her own eyes and sank back a little and offered it up. Her mouth. He'd put breath-odour on because he smelt not of food and kirsch but faintly of something from a chemist's.

'I can't tell you,' he said, when he released her, 'what this means to me.' The kiss was clumsy.

'But you have girls,' she said, 'reclining right now on your floataway chairs.'

'They're for ornament,' he said, 'I don't sleep with them. They're just dolls . . .'

'I'm a doll,' she said, and felt her stomach grow hollow with terror. She made a move by reaching down to grope for her sandals. He saw it at once and rose with her and offered his arm courteously as a balancer while she slipped the sandals on. He would not insist. She was warm and generous again. The minute she thought he wanted nothing she was able to flower, but if he reached out she closed and hardened.

'And you were married?' he said. Her third finger still bore the trace of the ring and had a small bruise where the ring had rubbed against it. They walked back in another direction so that she could see another part of the garden and inhale new smells. A white misty flower spread and sprawled over the rockery and gave a smell that she would always think of, rightly or wrongly, as the smell of orange flower. It was strong and sweet and so pervasive that it seemed as if the flower itself must do the merciful act of watering and rain sweet perfume on the dry stone and the dry, cracked, beseeching earth. The earth was thirsty because it was against the law to leave hoses on for very long.

'We were all married,' she said, slightly bitter. 'It's a habit.'

'I did it three times,' he said, as if he was congratulating himself.

'Do you remember any of them?' she said.

83

'I remember the first, she was a scientist,' and then corrected himself, 'a sexy scientist, mind you.'

'And what about her?'

'Well, her problem was that she hated organizing family life, so, I decided we'd have a conference every morning after breakfast, and discuss the day's menu and who would collect the children . . .'

He talked slowly and thoughtfully and he lost her attention quite early on. She'd wanted something special, some moment culled and delivered from all the gross hours of menu and money and daily cares.

'Now my second wife,' he said, 'turned into a nymphomaniac.'

'That's tragic,' she said but in an amused voice. They were on the last flight of stairs that led to the garden and she hurried on ahead, her hand trailing behind clasped in his, but all the rest of her fleeing.

'I shot her,' he said in a quiet, flat tone.

'Jesus,' she said.

'By accident,' he said.

'Of course.'

'No wonder you're dead,' she thought, and took the last three steps in one bound.

Chapter Eleven

The garden was completely deserted. She turned on him sharply to see if he had arranged it.

'Where are they?' she asked.

'I should know,' he said, sensing her anger. The table was in ruin and the record of the last castrated man groaned away. The homosexuals had put it on and it had obviously been played again by them or by someone else. He crossed over to the player and touched a switch. In the silent room her eye rested on the huge fish-bone that someone had dexterously extracted without breaking. It looked angry on the silver platter, the long fish-bone with its sturdy white teeth.

'I bet Bobby did that,' she said, wanting to utter his name so that in a second she could decently ask where he was likely to be.

'We have it done in the kitchen before they carry the fish through,' he said quietly but with a sting.

'Where is he, where are they all?' she said, looking round at the traces of them: georgette scarves, hardly-worn high-heeled shoes with a costly designer's name engraved in gold on their insides, Denise's charm bracelet with all its little attachments spread out flat on the table-cloth as if put there to tell a story. Someone had drawn pussy cats on the cloth with a red Biro pen and the ash-tray near by was stuffed with barely smoked cigarettes.

'Desecration,' she said, and remembered how the garden had first seemed the moment she entered it.

'He's retired, I expect,' Sidney said, and then with a bitterish grin, 'and probably busy now.' He moved around, clicking the various lights off so that the place was beginning to get ghostly with an emptiness that reminded her of a deserted ballroom where she'd once waited because the band leader had promised to come back for her, once he'd put his instruments in the car. She thought he'd hidden in the Gents and she waited behind one of the curtains that concealed a fire-escape, but later when she knew he was not coming back she moved tentatively over the slippery dance floor and tried to reconcile herself to disappointment. Then, as now, a wafer of moon lit the place but whereas then it had endowed her with loneliness, this night's moon was for this yellow, parched man who had killed his wife and hoped to sleep with her.

A figure came in from the hallway and she thought before she looked that it would be Bobby. It was Gwyn, come to say good night.

'Got to get some sleep so I can look pretty tomorrow,' she said, her voice slurred from alcohol.

'Sorry we had that little whatyacallit,' she said to Ellen and came across and kissed her pathetically.

'It's all right,' Ellen said, 'we were all a bit shaken.' She did not know what to say. She thought of the dead man again. Would the moon pick up the course of blood?

'Your stole?' she said then, suddenly remembering it.

'Forget it,' Gwyn said, and then for no reason and in a broken voice she said, 'Do you know, when we were first married we even had the same type of fountain pen, we were that much in love with each other.' She cried openly and like a baby and Ellen kept patting her and saying it was all right.

'Listen sweetie pie,' Sidney said, 'you've got to get some sleep so you can look pretty tomorrow for Jason.'

'Got to look pretty tomorrow,' she said, sinking into his arms as he led her away to one of the bedrooms.

'So,' he said returning and touching Ellen's elbow, 'Daddy puts them all to bye-byes.'

'Where do they sleep?' she said, meaning what trick of fate or manipulation has left me alone with you?

'Oh we got beds, we can sleep . . .' he paused, although he knew the number well, 'eighty.'

'Together or separate?' she asked, but he ignored the question and bent down and picked up an ear-ring from the marble floor. Looking into the jewelled leaf of its face he said, 'That must be little Suzie's, she had those for Christmas,' and he put it on a safe place under the mantel-shelf clock.

'Where's Gwyn's husband?' she asked.

'Oh he's around, he'll show up,' Sidney said. She wondered which of the slender sober girls he'd teamed with and how they actually got out of the room without questioning. Denise would be with Bobby for sure. The bracelet spread out on the table seemed to be a code saying, 'Gone with Bobby, gone with Bobby.'

'I must go home,' she said, looking around for her handbag.

'Don't say it, don't say it.' It was the first time he raised his voice and the first time a flush came in his cheeks.

'But I must,' she said quietly, her eyes damp from the tears shed on them by the other woman, her body worn out from the fierce exhaustion of hoping.

'Don't leave me,' he said. He was also saying, 'I am an old man and a sad one and nothing much quickens me any more and for some illogical reason you do, so stay.'

'Where would I sleep?' she said.

'You would just lie beside me,' he said. She shivered. There was something in his proposal that made her think of lying next to the dead.

'Do I have to?'

'You don't have to,' he said humbly. So humbly that she knew she must, and waving good night pointlessly to the empty room she went with him up two flights of marble stairs and entered a room with a door whose back and sides were covered in green baize so that it opened softly and closed again with the same hushed and sinister softness. She thought of a morgue. He pointed straight away to the bathroom leading through another doorway and she vanished there and took a long time over undressing. It was a big bathroom. In a large whisky vat there were soft stones of talcum powder, coloured a light mauve and smelling of stock in summer rain. She crumpled some and let them fall in the valley between her breasts and crushed some on her legs that were white where the sun lotion unevenly stopped, above her knee. She did this to, not to excite him but so that the light, mauve, summer smell might see her through. Far from being on the threshold of sin she saw herself as about to make a sacrifice.

He had already climbed into the enormous bed and was lying there in a blue nightshirt with a label that said 'All Action Garment'. She saw it as she stroked his neck.

'You found everything you wanted?' he said, ghastly polite. She'd found a bathrobe.

'Tell me what you like,' she said, 'your fetishes . . .' She was trying to be funny and trying to be loving but doing it badly.

'Hold it,' he said. As she did an enormous memory thirst took hold of her and she drank a tumbler of Perrier from the bedside cabinet.

'You want a drink?' she asked.

'No, little one,' he said, and thanked her for the hands that stroked and wakened him.

'Not for years . . .' he said.

'Don't think of it,' she said. If they got on to their

respective lonelinesses it would be unbearable altogether.

'You are a good person,' he said, 'kind.'

That sickly word.

'I'm a nurse at heart,' she said. 'Didn't you know that?'

'Nurse,' he said, mawkishly funny, 'can I have my medicine?'

'Provided you don't spill,' she said, mawkish too.

'Nurse,' he said, 'I'll be a good boy.' She imagined herself back as a student nurse, appalled by the occupation she had unwittingly chosen for herself. Doing the routine moves and saying the routine words, she remembered how she'd met her husband at a bus stop the very day she ran out of the operating theatre in terror and he asked why she cried. He offered to help her. Kindness. The most unkindest thing of all.

'You're a soft, soft woman,' Sidney said. Little did he know that it was his costly creams and his mauve talc that put the false softness and the false dew upon her.

'I'm glad,' she said, 'that it meets your requirements, sir . . .'

'You're so original,' he said, and then she lost the sense of the many senseless things he said and willed herself into a state of forgetfulness.

Afterwards she felt that she had failed him. She had wanted it to be a gift but it turned out hurried and nervous. Neither of them removed their clothes and she lay in the towel robe and he in the long, blue, 'All Action' nightshirt.

'I'll have to wash,' she said, soon.

'Have I made a mess on you?' he said, not even looking at her stomach, smeared as it was. He'd been a gentleman, he'd been careful.

'Just a little,' she said. She was thinking of egg white in its various stages of being whipped. He was telling the four-poster roof how happy and younger and glad he felt.

'Is there anything you want?' he said.

'Nothing.'

'A little trip, to some new place?' He was going to Marrakesh the following day for a few weeks.

'We're all going,' he said, 'a house party.'

'Bobby?' she asked, but not frantic now.

'I think we're all booked to go.'

'I can't come,' she said. He'd give her his card all the same and the day telephone number and the answering service at night in case she changed her mind suddenly.

'Can I sleep downstairs now?' she said abruptly.

'Something upset you?' he said.

'No, I just can't sleep with anyone near me.' She could not give him anything more, not even the solace of conversation.

'Of course,' he said, 'I'll move into the dressing room and you . . .'

But she was already out of bed and telling him truthfully that she wanted a bath and a little air and then to go to sleep on the garden hammock and be rocked by its gentle swaying. He must have guessed at her disgust because from the bedside desk he took a card and said,

'Put that in your purse.' It was the address of his house in Marrakesh and the various telephone numbers for the various hours of day and night. Reluctantly he let go of her hand and in the bathroom doorway she turned and closed her eyes and cradled her head in her hands to remind him that he must sleep.

She took a long time over her bath and almost enjoyed it. A second door led her out on the corridor and she found the stairs straight away. She went down slowly and noiselessly, on tip toe, her hand carefully clinging to the iron banister. Anyone would think she was being watched.

Just when she considered it light enough to leave, a

violet darkness descended on the living room where she had been resting. Then suddenly there was a ponderous clap of thunder followed by lightning so stark and green that she thought it was something electrically contrived. The huge window was open. More and more thunder followed, each clap running into the previous one like an enormous belch and the forks of lightning followed upon the thunder instantly. It was near. It seemed now that it had been threatening all night ever since they saw the dead man on the roadside, his blood flowing into the soft black tar. Then the rain came. Like stones pelting on a near-by glass roof and then coming in the open window, pushing the curtain ahead of it. She thought to close the window, but the intervals between the claps of thunder and the forks of lightning were not enough for her to get across the innumerable yards between where she stood and where the window was. The curtains were oyster silk with extra panels of silk like waves drawn across the width of each curtain. Within seconds the material was drenched grey and the waves were falling down laden with wet. The floor beneath was pooled with rain. It was not his black-and-white tiles she worried for, but getting the window closed for some more important reason as if a murderer were likely to come in.

'I'll do it after this flash,' she would say, moving a pace nearer and then ducking because of the next peal. The lightning in the room lit up a brown picture and made it sulphur green as if it were being painted anew. She'd never seen a storm like it. Half-way across the pavilion of the floor she sat down and knew that the curtains were now soaking, the floor under the window flooded and the furniture on that side of the room well drenched, so that there was nothing left to save. Remembering about metals she pushed an ashtray away from her and then pulled it back again because she was going to die anyhow. She remembered how as a child her mother had sent her sister in a storm all round the cottage shutting windows because her mother had wanted her sister to die. Her sister hadn't died then but had died another way, becoming a liar and marrying for money. They never corresponded now. Her death would be a shock all the same. She was going to die in this place and be buried God knows where. The colossal accident of her surroundings irked. She would have liked somewhere humble in keeping with her birthplace, the small council cottage with cliché, pink roses climbing up on either side. People used to say that she and her sister would go far because of their beauty. Black eyes, pale faces. She'd married above her mental means because of that startling face. Blackberries in an off-the-track Kerry road, he said, where there were no cars and no dust to blight the sheen on her. Marrying him she cut herself off, lost the knack of prayer, of superstitions, of going to dances and asking young men, 'Do you come here often?', of fierce friendships with other girls and linking and going for walks. She had to discard all those when she teamed with him because he was taking her into the fresh pasture of ideas and collective thought and flute music. It all sounded grand. Except that it wasn't enough and he didn't buoy her up when she hankered after the proverbs and accordion music and a statue of the Virgin hewn from black-thorn wood. When she admitted to these needs he put his hand to his mouth and swallowed painfully as if she had just farted sulphur. How superficial she was. The light-ning missed her part of the floor by inches and she waited now, patient and truthful, as she rarely was in life. What irony. She always thought he would die first, since he was older, and then the child would be hers exclusively. She knew many people in the world and would miss none of them except that child with its pre-aged face and the nice parts of her and the nice parts of him. Her flitteriness, his pensive ways. The only bit of her life she would re-live were the first few months of her marriage when her husband would make love to her on and off through the night and would afterwards talk to her with such words of sweetness that she was mesmerized as to how any man could love any woman so. And yet, it never being enough. She hungered for more: love, reassurance, as if what had gone in had been mysteriously drained away by some sort of spiritual diabetic flow. And if he punished her now with black looks it was because he knew she had not matched an eye for an eye and a tooth for a tooth in the deep, exacting algebra of love. The best part was over. It was a relief to die except for the fact of leaving a son. She looked down at the pad on the couch which said, 'Dear Sidney, Thank you for the pleasant evening,' and she tore it in tiny pieces rejecting its smarmy falseness now that she had only a few minutes left. Mindless of the rain, the swift green lightning and the powerful thunder she wrote, 'My dear and only son, I came here to work [a lie] and got killed by mistake.' But on re-reading it too disgusted her. The third letter was very conspicuously chirpy; it said:

How are you and how is George? Behaving yourself I hope, eating nourishing cereal and doing plops in fields (mind the horseflies), and remembering to sleep with your eyes shut and no comics under the pillow. I want to tell you a story, don't go away. When I was your age I got a shilling from a man going by on a tandem (Exp. a tandem is a bicycle made for two) because he asked me the way to the canal. I used to stand at the gate saying 'hello' to people. Anyhow when I got the shilling I went off to the shop where we owed a lot of money because my father was out of work (hammer toes he had at the time) and I asked the grocer to take the shilling off our bill and he told me, do you know what he told me, 'To go up the river on a bicycle.' So I kept the shilling. But I think the grocer had a lot of spunk in him to tell me that. And I want you to have lots of spunk in you and if you're going to do a good, do a big good and don't go offering shillings around because they won't get anyone far. Put this in your pocket along with the two hundred and forty-seven sweet papers that are likely to be there. Goodbye, your Mother.

She addressed it to his father's house and hoped when he grew up he would understand it. But almost as she licked the scented gum she heard the rain soften and knew that the storm was moving away, and she felt cheated of her death.

Chapter Twelve

She was lying like that, dropping off to sleep when Gwyn came in, in her stocking feet, walking unsteadily with her hands in front, groping as if it were dark. It was quite bright.

'Aren't there any cigarettes?' she said, and Ellen sat up and saw the face that had gone to bed early to look nice for Jason. In the penetrating afterstorm light her hair was thin and worn, like a cheap doll's wig with the scalp showing through. Repeated bleachings had weakened it. Her face, because of the effort gone into preserving it, looked far older than a middle-aged face should.

'There was a storm,' Ellen said, to account for ornaments knocked over and broken.

'Don't be funny, it was a hurricane,' Gwyn said, and looked around impatiently for cigarettes.

'Behind you,' Ellen pointed, and the woman turned and bent towards a low table where there were tipped cigarettes and kitchen matches. Holding the long match as a taper she trained it on the floor to see how far the water came across the room.

'Go call the housekeeper, it's like Venice in here,' she said, but Ellen made no move.

'And the whole goddam place smells of flowers,' she said, sniffing. In the freshness the smell of flowers came from the garden and there were flowers also in vases all around.

'Looks like a funeral parlour to me.' She wandered

from one vase to another, looking at the flowers' faces, trying to identify them. 'They lupins?' she asked. A small bowl of misty blue flowers had been put there, it seemed, to match the blue of a stained-glass religious figure on the wall. She looked up at it. 'Old Moses,' she said defeated. Then she saw the nylon birds and screamed.

'Holy Jesus.' Instinctively she put her hands up to protect her eyes and her frail cotton-wool hair.

'They don't fly,' Ellen said. They were small gay-coloured birds, made of cloth that resembled down. There were dozens of them throughout the room, perched on the rims of vases and window-ledges and on the curtains. Those on the curtains were hung so as to appear dead.

'Boy, do I need a drink.' Gwyn poured a very big vodka, added tomato juice and then ground pepper furiously into the drink.

'A little fruit juice?' she said to Ellen. But meant a drink.

'Too early,' Ellen said.

'You'll rue it, my girl,' Gwyn said solemnly as she raised her glass to nothing and drank as if she'd been parched. She drank it right down in one draught and made herself another.

'I don't want to get drunk,' Ellen said, peevish. Gwyn faced her, paused, ran her tongue over her front teeth and said, 'You want to know something?' For a minute it looked as if she was going to deliver a punch.

'Yes,' Ellen said, raising herself to kneeling position and balancing on the arm of the sofa.

'The secret of not getting drunk is to drink all the time.' She delivered the words slowly and surely as if it were the one thing in the world she was certain of.

'I mean it,' she said. 'The only time I fell flat on my face was when I went out to dinner and had two highballs, without having had a drink all day. I'd been out taking the goddam dog to the vet or something.'

'You fell down?' Ellen said, for something to say.

'What?' the woman said, her voice high and rasping now as if she were going to argue. Looking around again, she repeated, why had the whole place to look like a funeral parlour, and Ellen got to her feet, intending to leave.

'You didn't do Sidney?' the woman said, as if she wanted a quarrel.

'I beg your pardon,' Ellen said, but not calm enough.

'Well don't, 'cos he can't. He's not supposed to. He's got some, oh, he's got a puncture, right through the heart.'

'I've been down here, writing letters,' Ellen said, showing the envelope and then putting it in her handbag. The sooner she got out the better. Maybe he was dead. They would know, have tests carried out, trace her. She saw her name in all the papers. A wicked tourist. Her son would have to change his school.

'His lady-love shot him for ineffectuality,' Gwyn said.

'He shot her,' Ellen said. He had to be in the wrong. He just had to be.

'Poor lamb, he can't shoot peanuts,' Gwyn said, and let out a splutter of scorn. The wealth and beauty of that house turned to dust then and the cloth birds and the dirty pictures and the mystery people all shrank into tattiness and became the tatty props of a tired, dirty man, upstairs. All except Bobby, who had his own core of inviolate gutter-strength.

'Where's Bobby?' she said, the last question she would ask.

'Pretty nice, eh?' Gwyn said. She had moments of perception for all her foolishness.

'I liked him,' Ellen said.

'And he you. He searched around a bit for you

and then I guess he thought "Well, it's Sidney's house".'

'Sidney's house,' Ellen said bitterly. 'I must depart from you.'

She took a bunch of cigarettes for the journey and the rosiest apple from the fruit dish.

'What do you do, anyway?' the woman asked. A trick to hold her back.

'I work,' Ellen said righteously.

'You do?' said Gwyn, putting on a surprised look and forcing her eyes to open wide.

'And I was married,' Ellen said. She really disliked this woman.

'Was he darling?' the woman asked.

'Depends on your standards,' Ellen said, affronted. She didn't want to enlarge on it. She had claimed wifedom to give herself status, not to be cross-questioned.

'Jason's cute, I'll say that. Don't you think Jason's cute?' Not waiting for a reply, she told the sweet breath of morning air and the empty damaged room:

'Jason's sweet but I could kill Jason's mother.'

Then she sat down and sighed, and opened her purse with a snap. To a small, sharp-edged mirror she addressed herself.

'C'mon, how do I look, how does the lady look?'

'Jesus Christ,' she replied to herself, 'she looks like her eyes have been taken out and deep-fried or something.'

Ellen put her hands to her ears in a habitual gesture of withdrawal. Running again.

'Open your ears for Chrissake,' Gwyn said, and dropped the mirror on to her lap where she could refer to it between sips.

'So you're married and all that,' she said, looking at the tall girl in the blue dress shrinking away.

'Was,' Ellen said, sharp again.

'He fuck you, or not?' Gwyn asked. The question was

so sober and abrupt coming from such a rambling and blurred person that Ellen started a little.

'Two kinds of men, they fuck everyone or they fuck no one. All very sad,' she said, busy now with her nails. She was cleaning one set of finger-nails with their opposite counterparts. Her hands were long and white and soft. Hands into which cream and money had been poured and unlike the face they were able to be beautiful without showing the umbrage of the unloved. She had her eyes lowered, concentrating on her nails. Ellen took the last two vital steps to the doorway.

'Don't go,' the woman said, raising her eyes, pitiful, speechless. Like a runny-eyed spaniel. She spoke quietly: she had two voices, the tough rasping voice and the quiet salutary one.

'The first time it was with my best friend. He went up to New York and couldn't get a hotel, there was a ball game or something. I rang up in the middle of the night and I said "You get out of there".'

'And did he?' Ellen asked, trembling as if it had been her own husband and her own life that was at stake.

'Like hell he did. I didn't see her for months, then I went up to New York myself to get some shades and I called her from my hotel, I said, "Suzie I'm here," thinking she'd say, "Come on over," and d'you know she fixed a tea date for Thursday. Thursday! This was Monday! I couldn't believe it. She fixed it for some store because the tea was good and the cups. They were pure white china cups. I'll never forget them and they had this little scroll, this little gold thing, I guess you'd call it a flower on the inside and do you know I did the craziest thing after she left, I went down to the china department and bought a set of those cups.' She paused, and reverting to her tough, husky voice she said in answer to the question Ellen had not asked but had been thinking.

'Never mentioned it, neither of them.'

'You should have,' Ellen said.

'The hell I should,' the woman said, and went over and mixed two new drinks in two new glasses and gave one to Ellen. They were buddies now.

'And they kept seeing each other?' Ellen was gripped for a minute by the fiction of the woman's life.

'God for years,' the woman said, throwing her hand away as if she couldn't be bothered reckoning up the length of time.

'You should have . . .' Ellen said, about to deliver advice but the woman remembered something else and burst in with it. 'Someone advised me that if I wrote about it I'd get it kinda cleared out of me the way Jane Austen and people did, and I tried, and do you want to know what happened?' Ellen already knew or guessed but shook her head.

'It holds the door back between the kitchen and the terrace when I carry the dishes through on the maid's day off.'

'It can't be that bad,' Ellen said, trying to say something sympathetic.

'Oh let's not talk about it. I never bore people with my problems,' she said. They heard the footsteps.

'Well I'll be damned,' Jason said, as he stood in the threshold, wearing light-blue canvas trousers and a shirt that had the colour and texture of sand. Ellen stood back, to let him enter.

'There's my boy,' Gwyn said and put her hand out, and she rose and they made an arch with hands and their arms and he sang, in a false hearty voice:

'I will give thee a gold . . . en b . . . all,
  If you will marry,
  Marry, marry, marry,
  If you will marry me.'

Their morning offering.

And she sang:

> 'And I will take your golden ball
> If you will marry, marry, marry,'

and seeing that she teetered he lowered her arms and helped her to sit down again.

'Where've you been?' he asked.

'Oh having a little breakfast and a little talk. She's darling,' she said, pointing to Ellen, reverting to her little-girl voice now. 'I was jus' saying if she ever comes to New York she's got herself a friend. Hell she's got herself a friend anyhow. And you know that blue wrap I have with the fox collar –' she was gazing into his shifty eyes now, searching his face to know which of the little whores in slit skirts he'd slept with and how it had been – 'well it's hers when she gets to New York. Wouldn't it look cute on her . . . ?'

'It looks cute on you, Mary Pickford,' he said.

'Mary Pickford,' she said, affecting the deep husky voice now and laughing and pretending to be happy. Then pointing to the floor she said, 'Looks like we weren't behaving ourselves.' And he sniffed and she sniffed and said the flowers smelt kinda nice.

'You know what we're going to do today,' he said, and she looked at him with an obscene smile, licking her lips. He spoke very seriously:

'We're going to go out and get ourselves two fountain pens and you know what colour they're going to be?'

'Blue,' she said.

'Nope,' he said. Then his answer was delivered to the nape of her neck, marked from stretching itself too hard.

'Gold,' he said, 'eighteen-carat gold.' And they were so busy celebrating the fountain pens that they did not notice Ellen clutch her handbag tighter, wave a little embarrassed goodbye and slip away.

She took one look at Sidney, glad now that his door opened stealthily. He was as she left him, his eyes closed, his yellow face on the muslin pillow, the sheet folded back under his chin, laid out like a corpse. But he was breathing. Her own breath held, she listened joyously for his and smiled and thanked God for the narrow escape. She thought she might run into Bobby on the stairs but it was too early and not even the servants were yet stirring.

Outside under the rinsed blue sky the lawn and flower-beds were moist. But the road had dried off and except for the freshness in the air it would have been impossible to say there was a storm. She took the road that they had climbed the previous night, walking quickly at first. She kept hurrying to bends, only to see other bends a little ahead of her. Where the walls were high she lost the sea. Palm trees went straight up, higher than the walls, but the branches never interlocked so that there was no shade. Only the fig trees looked remotely like trees. The poppies growing out of the walls were crepe-paper flowers. Sometimes she plucked one and smelt it, then tore its paper face between her fingers. It was getting hot. On the prow of a hill she stood and unhooked her brassière. Down below, it was impossible to say how far below, she could see a village where she hoped to catch a bus that would take her back to her hotel. Already she felt better because she'd decided to go home that day. The feeling of disappointment over losing the actor had left her and the nausea of Sidney and the sadness of the sad woman; they'd all gone out of her life, she was safe, she was going home to her son. Sometimes she ran and then again she had to stand and catch her breath, but all the time she was making headway.

Chapter Thirteen

But it did not work out like that at all. After she got back
to her hotel she fell asleep. The journey had taken hours
between walking to a village, catching a bus to Cannes
and then waiting for another bus to her own town. When
she got back at noon the heat was brutal. Even the road-
menders who were black from sun looked up at it, apprehensive, as if it were going to burst over their heads. They
skulked under trees to eat lunch. The light was zinc,
shutters were being folded over to keep it out, shops
closing. The only cool things were the cool silk dresses in
the shop windows, under the awnings. Coming out of the
Travel Office, Ellen looked at them with longing, she
might buy one if she had enough money left. There was
no seat on the plane that day but if a cancellation came
through they would ring. Then she would pay her bill,
buy a toy for her son and if possible one of those lovely cool
dresses. There were little insects in the air. Outside a
restaurant a young boy went by with a spray gun, pump-
ing a liquid out. She could taste the chemical in her
mouth and that made her feel hotter still. He was a tall
boy with a curiously dazed expression and he did not
smile as she went by. She liked the boys who did not smile
at her. In a way she wished that he had.

Back at the hotel she undressed, lay on her bed and fell
fast asleep.

Wakened by a knock she came to, thinking it was her
son, and then realizing her surroundings she thought it

was the room-boy and put her hands across her breasts to guard them.

'It's me, honey.'

It took her seconds to recognize the voice as being Denise's.

'It's you, honey,' she said acidly. Her head pained and she had a terrible thirst.

'Oh come on, don't be mad at me, I didn't know where I was . . .' Denise said. Rather than have their night's history delivered in the corridor Ellen opened the door and let the girl in. She was wearing a grey dress and looked sober.

'Prodigal,' Ellen said.

'Honest . . .' Denise said and paused. Her voice was low as if she was talking in a church. Whatever occurred it had improved her face, given it back its childhood curves. Ellen felt a moment's gladness on account of this and a small smile escaped from her thin, boned face. How elementary the aids to happiness. Little liver pills. Winning money. But much more so, an embrace, or a proposition, or a night's panting. The great brainwash began in childhood. Slipped in between the catechism advocating chastity for women was the secret message that a man and a man's body was the true and absolute propitiation.

'So you're not mad,' Denise said, relieved by the smile. Ellen re-hardened. They must not get friendly or she might be obliged to hear the one thing that could stab her.

'It was just another of those stupid, crowd-scene nights . . .' Ellen said, looking abstractedly round the room as if there were something she had to locate. Oh for humility. Why could she not say that the gathering first enthralled her and later sickened her because her little-girl dream had not come to pass. Denise was rattling on:

'I looked for you and suddenly you weren't there, and then someone's bringing me up steps and more steps, it's like the Eiffel Tower only worse and I'm in bed stroking his hair and I'm saying, Frankie . . .'

'Who's Frankie?' Ellen said, caustic again. She was in charge of this girl as she never suspected she could be.

'Frankie's my . . . was my beau.'

'So you slept with our hero?' Ellen said. 'You could sell it to the magazines, call them long distance, reverse the charges . . .'

'Listen,' Denise said, less placatory now, 'stop it. I got the understudy, some slob . . .'

Whether it was true or not, Ellen felt enormous relief. She moved about now, taking dresses off their hangers, waving them saying, 'I'm off, I'm off . . .'

'I thought you were nice when I first saw you . . .'

'Nice?' Ellen said as if it were a dirty word. There was a long ash on her cigarette and she speculated how many minutes she could go without tipping it. She made a production out of just packing.

'Don't you want to ask me,' Denise said following her.

'You were raped,' Ellen said, 'and it was your father, sorry, your stepfather, and ever since when you meet men . . .' and as she talked she looked and saw the thick face weaken as if it were being pulped and she thought, 'How hard I have become, how hard,' and she stopped. The girl opposite her in the grey dress was on the verge of awful, humiliating tears. Ellen felt tears come in her own eyes, and they looked at each other and laughed a little behind their tears. Denise sat down. Ellen hid her face by delving into the suitcase. They would not cry. She spoke for them both. On the contrary they would have a drink sent up and they would drink to women alone, to women's solely noble hour without the company of men to vie for. She ordered two champagne cocktails and asked the operator to get the Travel Office again. She was really impatient to get home.

'You can't go . . .' Denise said. 'It's too soon, it's still August. August is the month.' She proclaimed it as if she was also in need of reassuring herself.

'The wicked month,' Ellen said, thinking of her own pathetic struggles towards wickedness. She could see Sidney's face close to death, on the starched pillow; and the violinist behind the camera stocking up with titillation for the winter months.

'I have to go, I have a son,' she said, for no apparent reason. And again, for no better reason, she added, 'His name is Mark but we call him Rock.'

'You're crazy about kids?' Denise asked, threatened.

'Not really,' Ellen said and recalled a story she had been told of a woman who locked her son into a bathroom and of the child subsequently boring a hole through the wall and Ellen herself asking very coldly if it had been a tiled wall because in that case the child's persistence was greater.

'I'm crazy about him, but nothing else much,' Ellen said, picking up clothes she had never worn and stuffing them purposefully into the fibre suitcase. Better to have bought a decent case. Her peasant origins coming out again. Caught napping.

'If you tell yourself you don't care, then you become like that,' she said, flatly.

'It's all slightly above my head,' Denise said. 'But what's your other name anyhow?'

'Ellen. Ellen Sage. Sage means wise or something like that.'

'I have a sneaking suspicion you're a nice girl,' Denise said as the boy knocked and came in with the drinks. They drank to that, to being nice girls, no matter what. They drank quickly and then as Ellen munched the cherry off the skewer Denise looked at hers and ran it over her face and said very abruptly, 'You got a guy then, or what?'

Ellen hesitated with her tongue between her lips. It was no longer possible to give simple answers to a simple question. There were tears in her eyes again.

'Don't cry, El, don't cry.'

'Who's crying?' Ellen said and snuffled. She would have to account for herself, say something, gloss it over. Denise put the pillow in another position and lay back as if she were going to hear a play. Ellen felt an impulse to summarize her life. She spoke quickly and in a voice that was unnatural to her:

'Irish, cottage, poor, typical, pink cheeks, came to be a nurse in London, loved by all the patients, loved being loved, ran from the operating theatre because one of those patients who had a cancer, was just opened and closed again, met a man who liked the nursemaid in me, married him in a registry office, threw away the faith, one son soon after. Over the years the love turned into something else and we broke up. Exit the nice girl.' She bowed on the last three words.

'It's marriage,' Denise said vehemently. 'It louses everything up.'

'It's not marriage, it's us,' Ellen said, she was weary of generalities.

There was a short silence. Suddenly feeling the heat, she let the cigarette fall from her mouth on to the wash-basin and ran the tap out of habit so as not to cause a fire. The telephone startled them both. The Travel Office people to say there was no seat for that day, but they'd made a reservation for the next day. She asked the time she was due to arrive in London and wrote it on her cigarette packet. She would buy her son a dinghy and a pump to blow it up, because if there was one thing in this world she baulked at, it was blowing up dinghies, or balloons. She would also pocket the little tubes of mustard and single-portion boxes of salt that they supplied with lunch on the plane. Her son would use them to play shop with George. She thought of Christmas again and how it did not matter if she never saw Hugh Whistler again. At least her journey had fulfilled its purpose in one way.

'But listen,' Denise said, jumping up, 'we have their house for the day, we'll go by and have a ball . . .'

'Who's there?' Ellen said. She had no intention of going.

'No one. They left in hordes, Sidney, the fairies, people I'd never seen . . .'

'Bobby?' Ellen said.

'God knows where he wound up last night, he was talkin' of going to the Casino when I last saw him . . .'

Ellen felt better already. A day away from the hotel meant money saved, not just the money spent on food and drinks and the innumerable cups of tea but the money that went towards such absurd things as tipping and the use of the bath. The man who held the bathroom keys was only willing to deliver them when he got a handsome tip. She thought of Sidney's bathroom, large, spacious with the soft stones of crushable talcum powder giving out a delicate lavender smell. Her greed mounted. She pictured again the various dresses in the shop windows and decided which one she would buy. Her mind was made up.

'Why not, see how the other half live . . .' she said. They would drink wine from lovely long-stemmed glasses . . . Denise was bubbling on about how they would have the pool and servants to wait on them and all of Mel Brooks . . .

'Do you know Mel Brooks?' she said. Ellen shook her head.

Denise looked annoyed. 'You haven't lived if you don't know who Mel Brooks is, I tellya, I know . . .' Already she was taking off her rings so that she could do her nails, before going over.

In the late afternoon they drove in a hire car through the town and along a country road. They passed two gold-stone houses and fields where women stooped as they harvested. The road was unfamiliar to both of them.

'It's going to cost several thousand dollars,' Ellen said, straining to see the meter.

'Maybe the guy's a killer, you never know,' Denise said, and then leaned forward and said to him, 'Excuse me, is this cab actually taking us where we want to go?' The driver made no reply.

'Every bloody one of those bloody French guys has something else in mind,' Denise said sitting back, winking at Ellen.

'I'm worried, honest to God I am,' Ellen said. She both was and wasn't. She half wondered if Bobby would be there, but talked about the driver and the heat lumps under her skin. Tiny red lumps. The more she scratched the bigger they got. Denise took hold of Ellen's small, white, peasant hands to stop her scratching. They were that friendly. An agreeable last day.

In the large downstairs window she saw the reflected image of the hire car as they drove up to Sidney's house. She and Denise got out together, Denise on one side, she on the other. They shared the cost of the taxi and Ellen hoped that no one looked. There was something shameful in carrying on money transactions and being watched. It cost far too much. But they had no chance to argue because the window was opened and Bobby came out in a white short-sleeved shirt. He said 'Welcome' as if he had been expecting them. Perhaps he had. Ellen suspected Denise at once. Had she invited her just to make it casual, or to humiliate her? Must she once again play plain, simple, old-fashioned gooseberry? He put an arm around each of them and led them through the open window towards the back of the house.

'You're just in time, I'm doing the marrows,' he said, and laughed as if he was engaged in something wicked. He looked from one to the other, smiling equally at both. Denise had a very wide smile. Her eyes were large, brilliant, brown in colour, fringed with long false eyelashes. They seemed to be smiling straight at him even though her face was in profile. She kept them wide open without blinking. Ellen could never fathom why it was that other women no better looking than herself made a better impression. She could look well talking to herself in a mirror or again talking to herself through the pool of a loving man's eyes, but most times she looked mawkish, and curiously unfinished.

'How long since your last Confession?' he said, commenting on the virgin starch of her shirt and the black silk skirt that came well below the knees.

'Oh she's full of the guilt jag . . .' Denise said.

'She knows me twenty minutes . . .' Ellen said in a hysterical voice. She hadn't prepared for this situation. Where was Sidney, where were all the others? The others, he said, were gone to Morocco, except for Gwyn and Jason and a few people who were gone riding. He was master of the house. They walked through one room and then another and out to the veranda and along a path bordered with flowers. His canvas shoes made no noise on the flagstones, but hers and Denise's were like armour clanking and competing with one another. The war was on. He had both their arms linked. In a few seconds they were in a glass-house. It was suffocating. The glass steamed over from the heat. There were flowers that looked unreal, big lurid blooms of red and mauve in big terracotta pots. She touched them just to make sure. They were real all right but they had no smell. The smell was of geranium leaves and tomatoes. She touched the wrinkled leaves of white geraniums and looked at their white unblemished petals. To smell the leaf and enjoy the petals, that would be the way to enjoy geraniums. The leaves in themselves looked pained. He picked one tomato, then another, and handed the girls one each.

'I'm not hungry . . .' Denise said. She really starved herself.

'Take it,' he said. 'It's great, it's right out of a tin . . .'

He watched them both chew and asked Ellen if hers was good. She nodded.

'Well have another, then.' He put it in her mouth and watched while she bit into it and some of the seeds spluttered on to her chin.

'Huh.' He wiped them off with his finger and licked it. Sober, he was perfect to be with. She wished in a way that she had not seen him again because she was getting soft and hopeful. All acceptance again. She thought of the previous night and how close they had come and she smiled. He saw it happen. He put his arm under her long hair and let it sweep his skin from the elbow to the wrist.

'You're like Cinderella or something,' he said.

'Or something,' she said modestly.

'Walk me to the subway,' Denise said putting her arm out for him to link, but not moving. He saw her pique and touched her lightly under the chin. In that moment it looked as if they had slept together the previous night. Ellen turned to the geraniums.

'And now for the mating rites,' Bobby said as he steered them both towards a trough where there were a lot of green leaves and small marrows of different shapes under the leaves. There were flowers too, yellow flowers, limp and tired looking but quivering with pollen. They drooped in the sun. He broke a flower very gently and brought its face to the face of another flower and let them touch very delicately.

'Clean fucking,' he said.

'Such nasty habits,' Denise said. She was looking very carefully. 'Do they enjoy it?'

'Does this always have to be done?' Ellen said enthralled. She had never seen such a ritual before.

'In nature the bees do it, or the wind,' he said, his fingers yellow from pollen dust.

'Or the wind,' she said longing for it. It was a special wind he conjured up: blowing pollen dust, sending seeds like velvet arrows to their appointed nests, scattering white geranium petals that fluttered like white butterflies; that wind in the tender blue inside elbows and thighs, no harsh sun, no Denise, the world soft with harmony and he and her joined together with fragments of wind like music falling upon them. It was too intimate, too physical a thought and she looked away. He stood straight as an arrow, his whey eyes saying to her, 'All right, I'll take you on.'

She looked towards his hands doing the wind's work, bringing the seed from one yellow flower to another. An act of creation. If I could put out my hand, she thought, but I cannot. Denise was there, saying, 'I quit America, I got a single ticket. I ended up in Scotland, cheapest fare, costs less to Scotland than anywhere in the world. Europe's for me, it's so goddam old, you know historic, you can live realistically, open up, grow, men treat you like a woman . . .' And already the simple moment had gone, Denise was speaking to him saying how men treat a girl and he was listening with a smile. The actor's downfall. He daren't lose a customer. Ellen felt hollowed again.

'Shall we take a walk?' he said, to Denise.

'Why not?' she said. They cantered off and Ellen followed a little behind. There was no telling how the evening would go.

Later they sat in the large room where Ellen had been earlier. She re-saw things as if she'd been away for a long time, the small gay coloured birds of nylon, the ear-ring under the clock, the picture that had been changed by lightning.

'I lived through a yellow thunderstorm here,' Ellen said idly, moving the ice around in her drink. He suggested they get stoned. But she liked him better sober. He had just been saying how he had always wanted to have two women together and this was his chance. Ellen looked at Denise with distaste. There was black blood in that girl somewhere. Their eyes met, they did not smile, but gleamed, the bare gleam of rivalry in their big eyes, her green eyes and Denise's brown ones. He was working his tongue in his mouth, the next thing he had to do was to spit. He stood midway between them, both hands on his belt as if guns were hanging there.

'You smoke like an amateur,' Denise said to Ellen who was holding a cigarette between her middle and her ring finger.

'And you're so observant,' Ellen said in a voice that people were accustomed to accept as real. A hard, formidable voice.

'And what are you going to do in Europe?' Bobby asked of Denise, pretending not to notice the duel.

'Well I can't give up acting, that's one thing,' she said. Up to that moment it had not been declared that she was an actress at all. It was quite touching the way she said it. Ellen watched him react. She tried to read the answer in the inclinations of his body. Then he suddenly walked as if he had made up his mind and sat on the sofa beside Denise.

'You're a good girl, sunshine, what else do you do?' he asked.

'I'm learning style,' she said, 'and writing . . . mainly for the discipline.'

'That's a Jesus brilliant thing to do,' he said.

'What's that supposed to be, an insult?' Denise said. She'd painted her lips a bit more. She and Ellen had withdrawn to his bedroom just before cocktails. Ellen had left her bag in there, by mistake.

'No joke,' he said. 'I admire you. I admire women who are on the ball.'

'Oh that's cute, you're getting so Latin, lover, what'll you give me . . .'

'Marshmallows of course,' he said. He punched at one of her breasts then the other.

'Hands off,' she said, and then looked at Ellen and said to him, 'She thinks we're stupid.'

Ellen was gazing into her glass of whisky, apparently indifferent to their flirtation.

'She's thinking what is the colour of the wind,' Ellen said, still looking into the glass, a half-smile of serenity on her face. It was not easy to keep so cool, but she wanted now to be the lone, interested observer.

'Egg-head stuff,' he said. 'All we want now is some very nice spiritual guy to make up a foursome.'

'That's where you're wrong,' Ellen said, smirking, tucking her feet up under her black skirt, drawing the skirt higher, very daintily with her thumb and first finger.

'I follow you,' he said, following the line of her very white, milk thigh beneath the darkness of the silk skirt. She'd decided not to use sun lotion. If her legs were white she was going to make a virtue out of it. Be the nurse she once set out to be.

At that moment a white-coated man appeared in the doorway and asked if they wanted anything.

'Dinner?' he asked, looking at Bobby, then at each of the guests. None of them responded to the question.

'Any pussy cats in the garden?' Denise asked the white-coated figure. He did not know what to say.

'Are there,' she repeated, 'any pussy cats in the garden?'

He said that he did not know and bowed slightly and excused himself. They went on sitting, drinking, once Bobby stood up to click on a light but Denise put her hand out to restrain him, she said the light brought the mosquitoes and if there was one thing in the world she was allergic to it was boring mosquitoes. He shrugged and sat down again. The distance between them on the couch was at least a yard. Ellen, who had been looking at a magazine, closed it and folded her hands and waited.

'You may not know it but you are still a woman in your wiles,' Ellen said. Spears of conversation like that escaped from her mouth.

'And under your armpits,' Bobby said, jocosely. Denise was dressed in a light-blue sleeveless dress and an arc of black showed when she raised her arms above her head and murmured something inaudible but cuddle-some.

Outside the night ripened. It was immense and black. They still sat. In the complete darkness only the paler things showed, her white shirt, and his, her pair of hands, their hands. She felt for her heat spots and scratched them violently. Crickets from the garden. Bobby and Denise got on to talking about old movies, ones she'd never seen. Ellen's eyes getting used to the darkness imagined that they were drawing nearer to each other. Two of their four hands went out of sight. Perhaps they had them clenched under his, or her, thigh. The conclusion being reached was that they loved Gary Cooper. Then Bobby stood up and walked with long strides towards the door, his white shirt disappearing into the greater darkness of the hall.

'For the sake of old times I'll show you the pussy cats,' he said. Denise stood up and ran, absolutely ran after him.

Ellen was not sure what she would do. Whether it would be something ridiculous and shameful or tragic and noble. For a long time she did nothing except sit there and think about ineptitude. Then she rose and decided to get her handbag.

Chapter Fourteen

They locked her out. She hung around the hall, her back to their door, not stirring, just waiting for sounds of them, and once again she thought, 'This is not me, I am not doing this,' and she remembered the calvary journeys her mother made across the narrow hall to her father's bedroom and the don'ts and the don'ts and the don'ts; she waited now, as then, knowing that the first sounds that would carry them heavenwards would also be the beginning of the end. She felt no humiliation, they would be empty for each other after and she would still be unexplored for him, and therefore desirable. To pass the time she began to fit on the hats. They were the hats left by each of the summer visitors. It was one of Sidney's little crazes, to have each person leave a hat on the big table. She tried first a linen one, then a straw one over that, then another straw that was wider, and lastly the very ornamental one with baubles, and dolls' mirrors stitched on its wide brim. She set herself little time limits. She thought, 'By the time I count a hundred, or put on four more hats or jump from the gold tile to the black spotted one' – there were many colour tiles in the big hall – 'he will have opened the door and he will be saying: "How 'bout us going drinking, ma'am?"'

Their light was out and from under the door came the sounds: the murmur and bed-creak and whisper of people in the dark. There were foot sounds soon after and a thud as if a shoe or a clothes brush had been dropped, and then it was quite still for a while as she tried to deduce what part of the ritual was over and what yet to come. Her bag was in there so she could not even smoke, and she daren't go upstairs in case they heard her departure and sneaked out. Not that they would. Anyhow she wanted to be there when they came out, smiling, disapproving, triumphant. She planned what she would say, she would say, 'Anyone for tennis?' and he, being as he was the first one likely to appear, would tell her to get her hair combed because they were going out and then the Princess would come, her hair all neat again but her dress a little wrinkled around the middle.

'It must be ten,' she thought as the clock from another room began to strike. The chimes were slow, steady, and friendly. She counted ten. A good omen.

Then in the lonely hallway where it was beginning to get dark she turned to face their door and reaching out put her hand on the brass knob that had the likeness of Sidney's face. In fact was Sidney's face. She held it for a while before turning it. If she turned it back and forth the inside knob – someone else's face – would move and one or other of them would see it and call out. Strange, how when the urgency was over people regained their embarrassment. Then she remembered that it was dark in there and they would not see the knob being turned, so she knocked on the door very lightly, and, in the light, inconsequential voice which she had rehearsed she said, 'Anyone for tennis?' They made no answer. She knocked louder and with her other hand she turned the knob and gave the door a little push. Through the narrow slit of darkness she said,

'I want my handbag.' They made no answer.

'Can you please hand me out my handbag?' she said, galled by their ill manners. She waited, knowing she could not retreat, and after a decent interval she pushed the door and entered the room.

In the half-light she saw the bed, the covers in a mound, then her eyes travelled farther up and she saw the empty dented shapes of big, square, white pillows and clicking on the light she saw how trespassed the bed had been and how empty it was. It was the emptiest bed she'd ever seen. They'd gone. The window was open wide and she remembered having heard the footsteps and the thud and she stood staring at the empty bed as if she could not think what to tell herself to do next. Then she flung herself on it, face down, hitting, pounding, cursing and crying with her fists and with her eyes, and when the temper had passed she lay on her back and pulled the sheet up over herself, and stretching and tensing her legs she felt the smooth, silk feel of the sheet over her.

When she was calm she got up and opened his bureau drawers. She picked out several silk handkerchiefs but just tossed them and threw them back, and his shirts were too big for her and the silver brush set was in such awful taste she would not be bothered to steal it. But she wanted to violate the place in some way. She thought, 'What can I do to this house short of burning it?' She passed water and left the lavatory unflushed and then drank liquor straight from the bottle and poured what she could not drink down a sink. She was ready to go. She dialled the operator to ask about a taxi and then she said, into the telephone, 'Do you speak English by any chance?' and so surprised was she when the girl said 'yes' that without having intended to she asked for her husband's London number. She would ask him to meet her at the airport. She would see her son sooner in that way and hand him the big present and hug him and they would all go out to tea. They might even get on well. He and her. They would compare holidays; she would hold back the sordid bit. Who knows, they might even look in each other's faces and see something they cherished. Rock would have the present on the table. He would eat several cakes. If possible she would pay the bill. They would be happy. Even briefly happy. As she thought this she was fitting on a blue suede jacket of Bobby's and wondering if she could have the sleeves shortened when the call came through and she heard two voices, one French, the other English, talking in French and then the English voice talking to her directly in English, and then to her amazement her husband at the other end saying,

'Where are you?'

'I'm in France,' she said, 'I was lonely so I came away for a little holiday.'

He was saying how he had put SOS bulletins all over England for her and she thought for an insane second that he had missed her so desperately he was calling her back, and then she knew that his voice was furious and she said, 'What?'

'Mark,' he said, 'got killed.' He never used the pet-name of Rock.

'What?' she said again. He must be out of his mind. She shouted at him to speak up, to explain himself.

'Where is he?' she said, not waiting for his reply.

'He got killed,' he said, 'on the road. A car ran over him.'

'God almighty,' she said. 'Why didn't you find me?'

'There has been an SOS out for you for three days,' he said. 'How were we to know you were vacationing?'

'Three days, where is he?' she said again. 'In hospital?'

'I told you, he's dead.'

'And buried?' she said, as if only by being buried was his death absolute. He said yes, buried.

'How could you bury him without me?' she said.

'Listen,' he said, 'it's not the time for feeling injured. I saw him, I was with him . . .'

'And why didn't you get killed?' she thought bitterly. She asked where he was buried.

'In Wales,' he said, 'where we were.'

'But how . . . how?'

'He went for the milk, he went every morning . . .'

'You fool, too lazy to go yourself,' she said, and thought hatefully of the various tins of plaster and the small useless bottles of medicine that he'd transferred from the larger bottles. A spume of hatred and blame fell out of her mouth and if there was one pleasure in the world that she could have relished at that moment it would have been the pleasure of being able at last to blame him for the most terrible crime possible. Their roles at last reversed!

'Listen,' he said. 'Listen, listen.'

'You killed him,' she said. 'You did it, it was your fault.'

'Thank you,' he said, 'for your charity,' and she knew it was awful for him too and she felt a little sorry. 'How bad was it?' she said, in a different tone of voice.

'I never saw him,' he said. 'They had to cover him up.'

'Who covered him up?' she said. That should be something only she could do.

'A road-mender on his way to work.'

'Was his head . . . ?' she asked, not daring to bring herself to use the word split.

'Everything,' he said, 'was mutilated,' and she knew without asking that he'd possibly been put into the coffin like that with the blanket over him holding the mutilated parts together.

'Who was at the funeral?' she said. The questions came automatically. They were not the questions she wanted to ask.

'I was,' he said, and she saw him before an open grave in a black coat, standing there for ever. The operator butted in to know if they were finished and she shouted no and asked him for God's sake to tell her, to tell her everything, to stop making it worse by having to be asked every single question.

'Do you think I'm able?' he said. His voice was pitiful.

'I'll come back,' she said. 'I'll get a plane tonight.'

'I don't want to see you,' he said. 'You're the last person.'

'But we *have* to help one another, we have to,' she said.

'Don't come,' he said. 'I couldn't see you,' and then he told her he was going to ring off and he did. She realized that he had not asked where she was or anything about her. He was serious when he said he did not want to see her. She put the telephone back and stood absolutely still.

It is always thought that in times of crisis people go wild, but she was not wild. She was calm and able to say to herself that she had killed her son. The logic was simple: if she'd never left her husband they would have holidayed together and she and the child would have gone for the milk and they would have stood, hands held, waiting for the car to go by and it would be something that flashed by leaving a cloud behind and they would have then crossed the road.

Her hand had moved with the thought. It was opened out to grasp his, and looking at it empty she felt the first bit of physical torture that was to be the beginning of knowing he was dead. She held his face, his little neck, kissed his hair that was cut like a monk's and pieced what she saw before her eyes with what her husband had said and she was not so calm then. She had to do something. She rushed through the room and corridors and past other rooms to where the servants were and told Antonio in one unhalting burst. He did not understand fully, but his dark, dour face darkened more and he stood up and gave her a drink of water and called his wife who was looking at television in the other room and his wife got the sense of it at once. Then there were a lot of footsteps hurrying along corridors and servants she'd never seen came to attend to her and she was given drink and put in a chair and out of nowhere Gwyn and Jason appeared with two other people, all of whom embraced her. Being with all these people helped because they were so strange and far away and they gave her mixtures of drink and pills that blurred what they said and what she told them. There was some talk of chartering a plane that night.

'You'd better ring him,' she said to Jason and gave him her husband's telephone number. Jason was away for quite a while and when he came back he said it would be better not to charter the plane. Obviously he'd made the telephone call and found her husband as hostile as she had found him. Jason kept saying it was an accident, a lousy accident. Someone asked stupidly if the name and number of the motorist who had killed the child was known. This practicality sent a shiver through them because they remembered the dead man on the road and how dead he'd been and how pointless it was to have his murderers standing by.

'I don't want to know who killed him,' she said. They agreed, they said it didn't pay to seek revenge. They gave her 'Sweet-Dreams' pills from a big bottle thus labelled and they moved in groups from room to room, searching out new chairs and new positions so that they could all be comfortable.

'He was always on to me to get goldfish,' Ellen said. Her son, she meant. One minute she was talking about that, one minute about her husband. Someone asked was he nice.

'He looks sadder than he is,' she said, but did not know what she meant. She began talking about her child again

123

and told how he'd taken fright at a new frilly bedspread and cried out and said, 'It might turn into a lady in the middle of the night,' and then there was some rambling generalization from her about inherited groundless fear. Everyone nodded. Heads shook. They knew in their half-drunken senses that this time her fears were not groundless but had happened.

'Death was never absolutely real before,' she said. Her mother had died, of cancer, her father had died soon after, of neglect. She'd buried them, had a novena of masses offered, paid for the coffins, the hearses, and the barrels of porter drunk at their wake, cried, worn a black diamond on her sleeve and remembered their possible Purgatories in gloomy November, the month of the Holy Souls; but those deaths were merely something sad and uncomfortable, going on outside her. Her son's was in her like a lancet, like a pain, she couldn't stand it: she screamed. They converged on her again, pills, whisky, arms on her shoulders, a basin in case she was going to be sick, towels, cold-water compresses, perfume, a rosary from Gwyn, a cold crucifix brought to her lips. Somehow they got through the night. Spells of calmness and then an outburst and people running back and forth. Nobody had any sleep.

'How old was he?' It was morning and they were all seated at a breakfast table. She saw egg yolk spewing down the side of a silver egg cup.

'Seven . . .'

And that was all anyone could say.

A while later they asked what they could do and she made a gesture that signified she did not know. When the cloth was removed she did not rise, nor did they, and she looked at the satin-wood table and thought how long it would be before they would grow tired of condolences and offer to take her back to the hotel and then on to the airport.

'What can we get you?' they said. 'Flowers?' and although she shook her head and meant no, they sent flowers later that day after they had carted her back to her hotel. She wanted to go back, she said, to stay in the hotel for one night to live it out, alone.

'She wants to be alone,' they said and she knew they were weary of keeping vigil with her. Anyhow what could they do? The flowers came. Two enormous bouquets: white flowers and blue flowers. She imagined they'd put some thought into it and they did not want these flowers to look gay. She placed them on the bed and saw them as wreaths, although they were not circular-shaped.

'Dead,' she said to Maurice the room-boy, who stood looking at the flowers on the bed but could not understand her tears.

'Enfant,' she said, and cradled a child in her arms so that he would understand. He stood looking at her but he did not know what to say. He'd come with whisky. Two glasses of it. She took one glass and began to drink. He stood watching, his hands folded. Then he picked up her suitcase, asking if she wished to leave soon.

'No,' she said, shaking her head, 'I'm not going.' It was too much trouble to explain that they'd buried the child, that there was nothing to go home to. After a while he left, backing out of the room nervously, as if he were frightened of being imprisoned there. She opened the window fully, then pulled at the cords until the shutters fell down and darkness flooded the room. She undressed and got into bed and drank from the second glass of whisky. She did not have to drink it all. The pills and the crying and the previous drink made her head swim and soon she was in a fevered sleep. It was not until the paper thudded through next morning that she stirred. Thick with hangover, and muddle she opened and read:

NUNS IN TAKEOVER BID
DEADLOCK IN THE BANANA WAR

First memory returned and then grief: as if in sleep she had thrown off the agony the way she'd stepped out of her uncomfortable shoes. The thought of England and of having to go home sent a cold shiver of terror through her. She bundled the paper in her hand, crumpling it so that it would be impossible to read at any hour of the day, and she reached for the drink left from the previous night and rang down for tea.

She did not pack or go home that day either. In the afternoon she forced herself to get up and go out and then impulsively she asked in a shop where it said 'Ici on parle anglais' if there was a Catholic church near. For she clung with her expiring virtue to habits like that. It was a small church with palm trees around it and the side door was open. She knelt for a while on the tiled floor near the water font, blessing herself over and over again with the Holy Water, saying 'Lord have mercy on him', each time. It was cool in the chapel and difficult to understand that outside the summer world still went on, the bodies still offered themselves up to the sun, car seats roasted, shutters were being closed, towels put out on balconies and the snow on the mountains beyond blindingly white. Her praying was automatic: it meant nothing. It was to make faith come. But no relief descended from the blistering heavens and she arose with grazed knees – sand had been walked into the tiles – and a vague feeling of having committed sacrilege for having prayed at all. She ought to bestir herself and go home to England, but her limbs were like lymph and she could barely drag herself around.

Chapter Fifteen

And then a strange thing happened. She entered the false lull that sometimes follows upon shock. She did not go home. She did not want to go home. By staying there she did not have to face calamity. She neither thought her son was dead nor was alive. She thought nothing. 'I'll stay one more day,' she would say, and mean it, but next day she was uttering the same thing. It was like being another person. She did not struggle. In the numbness of her flesh she could feel no reaction except a new and fanatic urgency to get sunburnt. She was the first out each morning, hurrying through the twilight of trees to sink on to the mattress which she had permanently booked. A few feet from the water. She had only to stretch her toe for the water to curl over it. An Arab with treacherous black-eyed cunning went by selling goat-skins, but never troubled her; another man came with dampened red roses in tight bunches of probably a dozen, and a third carried English papers and called out their names, but she bought nothing. She said nothing. When the English group smiled at her she looked abstracted. The woman with the lorgnette had grown tired of propositioning. They were merely living ghosts to Ellen. She'd bought new sunglasses with deep-blue tinted lenses and the effect was like being enclosed and swimming in an underground grotto with the soft noise of eddying water to lull the senses. No trouble from people. Once the glasses slipped down on her nose and she caught sight of a Scottish girl with a black crescent on her pink and freckled arm where teeth had sunk in. She'd seen the girl hover around the violinist in the lobby at night and heard her address him in garbled French. When Ellen saw that bite she felt distaste and, recalling the crudeness of day-to-day encounters, she quickly restored her glasses, retreating back to the safety of her grotto. The sun, the numbing sun was all she craved. Stretching her legs full length she would close her eyes and let it soak into her and pray for it to get stronger and stronger so that all the other people would flee and it would focus on her alone. She believed other people's presence was taking some of the fire from her. It was not enough that her outer skin should be burnt, she wanted it to penetrate right through her, to flow into her limbs as pure fire and become part of her energy. She talked to no one now, she looked at no one; sometimes through her lenses she would see people going by, shadows that came between her and the sun, and she never even speculated whether they were men or women. Gradually she altered. Her skin changed to red-gold, the colour deepening each day and at night she would go to sleep thinking only of the morning and the next day's baptism of fire. She ought to be feeling sad. She ought to be going home. She ought to be weeping. But she refused to think outside the environment of white, wan, listless-making heat.

Sometimes of course thoughts forced through, like damp seeping through stone walls or weeds bursting out of a slate roof. Then it hit her. She saw him, felt him, heard his voice:

'The most bloodthirsty animal is one and a half inches long. It is the common shrew.'

This and many scraps of knowledge like confetti fluttering around in his busy scatter-brain. They all spoke to her. A succession of his voices as they changed through the years: when he couldn't pronounce R, the lisp when he lost a tooth, the big, portmanteau words he loved, whispers of little feats to George in bed at night. The time he'd said, 'George is having a high and mighty piss contest,' and checked her face to find traces of anger, and seeing none went on repeating the word 'piss' with the jubilance possible only to the very innocent. She had horror images of his body in pieces all over the road and his arms wrenched off and thrown there. Then in her mind she would try screwing the arms back on as if they were dolls' arms. Piecing him together.

But that was to be expected.

On the whole she managed. She ate quite well and did not over-drink.

One late afternoon as she lay on the mattress, she felt, though her eyes were closed, that the someone standing over her was not one of the passing people. She stiffened. Her husband. Catching her out. How could she sit up and say, 'I am not malingering, I am getting some strength before I come face to face with it,' and looking through her lenses she saw that the man's face looming over her appeared to be smiling.

'So there you are,' it said. She recognized Bobby's drawl.

'Oh you,' she said, and sat up, neither pleased nor displeased.

'Thought you were in a ... ?' she didn't finish the sentence.

'Full o' fairies,' he said, sitting next to her.

'You look all right.' He pushed the straw hat back on her head so that he could see her face clearly.

'I feel all right.' She was grateful to him for not asking why she hadn't gone home.

'Nice place,' he said. He looked around and made faces at the bored, expectant girls, glistening with brown come-hither jelly. One stood up when she saw him and walked slowly past. He looked her up and down and said as she went by, loud enough for her to hear:

'Hail, the performance of the arse. Seats in all parts . . .'
She strolled to the sea and perched herself on the neck of the white gondola that was a few yards out. As if riding the neck of a swan.

'Waiting for a squitter,' he said, waving out to her. She did not wave back.

'You have a one-track mind,' Ellen said, but she was glad of a little conversation all the same.

'Who?' he said, and laughed. Then in an effeminate mincing voice he recited:

> 'But I do like to pee beside the seaside
> I do like to pee beside the sea,
> And I do love to pee inside the seaside
> With someone peeing in me . . .'

The English group manned by Arthur heard this and rose huffily, to leave. It was early for them.

'You're driving people away,' Ellen said. The English wife dressed her husband as Ellen had seen her do each day. She helped him into his shoes, his underpants and then his shorts. He'd graduated to wearing shorts.

'Jesus, man, where's your genital pride?' Bobby said, aiming the pistol of his finger at the helpless husband.

'You haven't told me about Tangier,' Ellen tried to engage Bobby, 'and Denise.'

'Fuck Denise,' he said, and rested his head on the floor of the beach to have an under view of the man who was being dressed.

'It's there,' he said, gripping her arm but looking in the direction of the English group. It was as if he had set himself a bet over it. 'The member is present all right,' he said, and then in a downcast voice, 'but not waiting to strike,' and burying his face in the sand he groaned and wallowed there.

'You're gone,' she said. When he sat up his eyes were closed and his sand-encrusted face a mask of what it once was. Sad and pained now, he held her hand and asked again how she was.

'Did you come to see me?' she asked.

'Of course.'

'Why?' But she knew why.

'They didn't tell me . . . I didn't hear about it for three days, then someone said . . . well someone said it.'

'Sometimes I don't . . . believe it,' Ellen said. He squeezed her hand and told her to talk or not to talk whichever she preferred and they sat like that, looking out to sea, and there was not a puff of wind. He brushed the sand away from the corners of his eyes but left the grainy mask over his face.

'Someone called it azure snot,' he said, 'Rimbaud, I guess. Only poet there was.'

'Called what?'

'The sea, you goose,' and then, very alertly, he flicked his fingers and asked, 'Goose, what do you think of, quick?'

'Potato stuffing,' she said.

'Jesus, women have no logic,' he said. 'Ask me one.'

'The colour of a road?' She flicked her fingers as he had done.

'All colours, ma'am, but I liked them gold.'

'What do you remember from when you were small?' she asked.

Something about his voice had put that golden road in a childhood sequence.

'Little sister gettin' done, saw it through a keyhole.' He closed one eye again and screwed up the other. The English group had departed.

'And peaches,' she said, 'falling apart.' The thought of anything falling apart now put it back in her head, the image of the way her son died. He put an arm around her.

'I have kids,' he said. 'Never see them.'

'Why?' she said, accusing.

'Their mother thinks I'm a wolf.'

'Are you a wolf?' She knew she was going to cry.

'I'm a wolf, I'm a wolf,' he said and snapped at her with his strong white teeth and then he cradled her in his arm and let her cry. Sometimes he made a joke about people going by and said she was missing a ball because corruptions were quickening all over the place. Sometimes he just patted her and then again he'd say,

'Wow, if people on the set could cry like you.'

She cried and spoke in senseless bursts and blew her nose into a towel. One minute she was saying: 'He put his clothes in a paper bag at night to save them from the moths,' and then she was describing how he cut his own hair and got sorry and tried to stick it back on with Sellotape before she saw it and that made her cry worse, and when she remembered, she apologized for blowing her nose so much. For no reason at all she began to talk about turtles on an island in the South Pacific. She said: 'Their mothers lay eggs in the sand and then they can't find their way back to sea and they wander all over the sand delirious and crying – turtles cry – and the children are born and they wander too, and they never know one another and they're all crazed and wandering.' There was some point to the story but she forgot it.

'The century of hell,' he said, in a low, even voice and for a minute she gave a thought to his children and asked how many they were and what sex.

'You'll have another kid,' he said. 'Or you'll have something?'

'How do you mean?' she said. Had he come with the intention of sleeping with her?

'*You* know,' he said. 'You've seen things – pretty things – come out of slums and slag heaps and manure heaps; you see those big, indiscreet trees?' He pointed to the palms behind the dressing rooms.

'They *are* indiscreet,' she said, through her tears.

'Something will come,' he said. 'Some sort of . . . You might get to be a gipsy like me.'

'I'll never get over it,' she said, affronted.

'No one's asking you,' he said, and then he rose and pulled her up by the hand and said,

'We need some liquor and fortification after all this high-powered talk and stuff . . .'

Going up under the trees towards the hotel she blew gently to get the last traces of sand off his face, and then she asked if she could change into another dress. She really wanted to bathe his eyes, because they looked bloodshot.

'We'll buy you a dress,' he said, and grinned. In the hotel boutique he bought her a costly white dress with a purse to match. The dress was made of linen, with big sleeves in which her hands could nestle. Like the saints that appear in the liturgy of the Church: white and limbless and very still.

'It's chastity day,' he said as they sat in the hotel, drinking a white frothy drink that he'd had specially made. He ordered four drinks each time because it took the barman some time to make them. In that way they were never without a drink. They were called daiquiris and there was rum in them, but because of their froth-like appearance they looked harmless. Sometimes he reached out and touched her hand or let his fingers travel up her arm under the mantle of white, but the touch was delicate, like the ineffable touch of winds. Suddenly she missed the wind and wished she could hear it blow.

'You cheer me up,' she said.

'Eye-wash.'

'You do.'

'I carry pessaries around,' he said, 'pessaries to cheer women up.'

'You're never serious,' she said.

'Serious!' he said as if she had just uttered an obscene word. 'Jesuses and Virgins, who wants to be that?'

He would not entertain any talk about his wife, his children, his friends, pictures he'd been in or pictures he was going to be in. Now and then he concentrated for long enough to tell her the exact taste and texture of a melon he'd had in the Arabian desert, its name and the superstitions attached to it. The melons he described had long, descriptive names like the names of Chinese poems. He talked about the light on the stones in Greece and how it changed as one drove by, and what it was like to be one thousand leagues inside the world's most sinful woman.

A little blurred from the drinks, mesmerized by his voice and his way of touching her thin arms under the wide, sacramental sleeves, she heard everything he said and did not question it, even when he said preposterous things. It fell dark outside, people passed through to dinner, and still he did not show signs of moving. The waiter brought almonds with the fresh drinks. Bobby gave big tips. Like her he wanted to be thought generous, and yet he insulted people.

'Are you *the* Bobby So-and-So?' asked a man going by.

'I am a Bobby so-and-so,' he said, and nodded to the waiter to take the man away. She stirred her drink nervously with a rod. There was a thin wooden rod for stirring, and a heart-shaped ashtray with three gold hollows on the rim for three cigarettes, though there were only two of them. Sometimes she looked in the wall mirror to see him talk to her, and his talking and her listening became half-dream, half-happening because of the awful silence of five days, the strong rum drinks, the love he shed on her. They were at a table near the window, the light outside a dark impenetrable blue. It did not seem like the same hotel where she'd met the violinist. He just went by and stared at her in an unseemly way. She felt triumphant that he had seen her with a man. A display of flowers at her back worried her hair and, leaning over, Bobby plucked one and put it under her armpit. The violinist saw that too. She held it tight, tighter, crushing it under her arm, thinking that perhaps its red dye might harm her new pure dress, thinking, but not over-worried.

'Your turn, ma'am,' he would say and look at her. She could say anything she liked. So long as she didn't talk serious or ask questions about his life.

'My knickers getting wet in a field of barley,' she said. Sensation for sensation. He'd given her the white peaches.

'A holy hour in a lavatory with a strumpet,' he said.

'Chamber pots never rinsed,' she said, and thought again of her home, the two bedrooms, wet clothes slung across the indoor line, the table never fully cleared off, relish bottles, relish stains, the garden as the lavatory.

'Keep it clean,' he said, and feigned anger by raising his fist.

'Wild garlic sweet on the breath,' she said quickly. They were playing a child's game and to miss one's turn was to fall out of the game. There was garlic in the hedges that boundaried the barley fields. And 'Please do not trespass' signs. And she herself not much higher than the high swaying barley ears. The landlords responsible for the 'Please do not trespass' signs could hardly distinguish her. She was blonde, also. It was later in life her hair darkened to red-gold.

'Good,' he said and rose and stretched himself. She put

the pressed flower in her new purse, and left a drink untouched.

'Look,' she said, showing the satin inside of the purse, 'it's clean.'

There was a car waiting for him outside. The driver handed him a telegram, but he didn't open it.

'Open it,' she wanted to say, 'in case you have to go,' but as they got into the back seat he stuffed it in his pocket. His tie billowed out from the draught caused by the open windows and she saw the label of a Paris fashion house.

'*Grandeur*,' she said. He took the penknife, the same one that he had used to cut the hairs off the artichoke, and sawed the label off and tossed it through the window.

'Someone else will find it and stitch it on,' she said.

'I don't care, I really don't care.' It was a thing he said often as if he had to assure himself of his indifference. They drove to a castle that was also a restaurant and he asked the driver to come back at midnight. The stone entrance arch was covered with vine and bell wistaria and there were a few flowers still in bloom, their light mauve phalloids hung limply over the green soft leaves. Like a man and a woman after loving. It was well known for its pictures, he told her, and very solemnly he walked her through the stone passage and from room to room to see the various paintings hung in dark gilt frames with tubular lights above each one. The rooms were dark but she could see the pictures quite clearly. Her favourite was of a drunk but thoughtful woman at a café table. Not joking now, not saying anything except a surprised and marvelling 'Christ' from time to time when he saw something that staggered him.

They ate out of doors and a huge black dog rested at their feet.

'It's the devil,' she said, 'keeping us apart.' The dog was between them under the stone table.

'You got the story wrong, ma'am, the devil is the guy who brings us together, it's mean old . . .' He looked up. The sky was vast and calm, its deep-blue light protective over them, and over all the holiday sinners. His mouth full of wine, he gluggled up at it and it seemed as if his laughter and his happiness vibrated on the leaves he looked through. In a seizure of happiness, she said:

'It's the nicest night I've ever had.'

And for that little minute she did not feel guilty for being happy so soon after her son died. Even when he was alive she was only a mother some of the time. She doted and hovered over him for months and then of a night she would have a wild longing to go through the town and do delirious things and not bear the responsibility of being a mother, for hours, or days, or weeks.

They had *crudités du pays* to start with. They were brought on a huge dish, and were of so many kinds of vegetable that she giggled about a garden having been wheeled through. There were two eggs also on the dish, their brown shells glistening, where they'd been buttered. He cracked one deftly on the stone table, held it over his mouth and swallowed it whole. She burped over-genteelly into the sleeve of her new dress. She could not stand eggs.

'Come on, eat,' he said. He knew the best sauce to dip each separate vegetable in and he chewed until he had robbed each mouthful of its flavour.

Afterwards they had a Châteaubriant steak and the wine that came was in a very old bottle with a cobweb round it.

'We never swam,' he said, as they recalled the day and how they'd passed it. 'We'll swim tonight.'

'I can't.' Better tell him than have to stand shivering in a bathing suit and disappoint him.

'You can't swim!' he said. She nodded. He would teach her the next day. She touched his hand lightly in gratitude. She thought again of the young priest that had once saved her from drowning and now, looking at Bobby, she thought of his greater gift to her. He'd given her forgetfulness, a day's distraction, a day's healing. When she remembered her son at all it was a sweet memory of his living another life, with real children, in a place she called Limbo. In a sense she inhabited Limbo too, a place of almost-painless, patient consciousness through which other thoughts from her other world wandered. But her son was in a happiness place. She'd had him secretly baptized as a baby and she had a sneaking relief about that now. Not that she believed or disbelieved, she simply did not know.

'Is there an after-life?' she said, quite ordinarily.

'There's half a glass each,' he said, holding the wine bottle firmly and taking the cobweb in his grasp. Afterwards she thought the cobweb got on his face because he wiped his jaw from time to time of some nuisance.

'Is there?' she said, looking towards the sea, made vaster by the darkness.

'What about the snails that have their heads cut off and grow new heads, what about that?'

'What about it?' she said. Had her fearfulness disappointed him? He wound a corner of the napkin round his finger and removed castor sugar from the valley at one side of her mouth. Detaining his hand with her cheek she looked at his arm in the white shirt and then at the tiny rim of dirt in the fold of the cuff.

'Dis . . . gusting,' he said. She was never to forget how he said that.

He booked a room in her hotel, to be there for the morning for her first swimming lesson. The biggest compliment anyone could have paid her.

'I'll be down in the lobby,' he said, 'so don't worry.'
They were on the threshold of her bedroom, the door half
open but the light in the room not on.

'Bobby, Robert,' she said. She wanted to kiss him,
thank him, make known to him with all of her five senses
how perfectly the day had gone.

'Get sleep,' he said, whispering because it was late, and
then, as she lingered, he took out a tiny silver pen and
wrote on her neck where the new dress had a diamond
opening. She looked down to read, but the scroll was too
close under her chin to see.

'See ya,' he said, and put the pen as a token in her new
purse. In the bedroom mirror she saw what he had
written:

QUEEN OF HEARTS

It was still there in the morning.

Early next morning she had her first lesson. He bought
rubbers for her arms and while he was blowing them out
he told her to go and make herself known to the sea. The
beaches all around were empty except for the sounds of
children. She hated the sounds of children now and put
her hands to her ears instinctively.

'Go on,' he said, 'baptism by water . . .'

It looked so simple to walk in. There were no clouds
written on the water. It was still cool, and a mist shrouded
the places all around and as far as she knew there was
only him and her. Coming into the sea he took her hands
and forced them both to duck down and douche their
bodies, then rise up and shake the water off their faces. He
said she must first get used to the water going in her eyes.

'Your hands,' he said again, taking hold of her and he
moved away until they were at arm's length. It took a lot
of persuasion before she risked raising her legs from the

sea-bed, but when she did, she clung tenaciously to his hands, and declared the most extraordinary trust in him. She could live like that for the whole of her life, his hands holding her, his beautiful happy eyes beholding her, her legs and body lost, but safe.

'Kick, kick, kick,' he would say as she moved towards him and he moved an equal distance away.

'Kick as if you were kicking a man,' he said. They laughed and stood for a while, and in the water he embraced her, a thing he had not done on land.

'We'll stay here for ever,' she said. But he said no. The first day she couldn't overdo it because her limbs would tire. True enough when they did come in and lie on the mattresses her legs ached and her stomach felt as if it had just been put to the first use in its whole life. They swam a couple of times more, and once they dried off with the sea water on them and another time they stood under the tap and he washed her all over and washed her hair even though she didn't wish that. Then he swam out alone and she kept looking for him but lost him among all the other swimmers. They lunched on the beach and afterwards he got the driver to take them up to the mountains. They went to a town where the shops sold only pottery. Vacant lots were strewn with yellow rubble, stone dust got in the back of the throat, and looking at some dying broom in front of houses she yearned again for rain, and the sight of cold violets overwhelmed by strong rain. They walked up and down the streets comparing the different pots in the different windows and with so much to choose from they ended up buying nothing.

He came every day then to give her a swimming lesson and afterwards they would lie side by side, hardly talking. Sometimes he would ask if she wanted anything and she'd reply with, 'We're lucky, aren't we?'

'We're sneaky,' he'd say, or smile or wink or just turn

her hat around so that the back ribbons dipped over her face.

'And it's not over yet,' she'd say, and to that he always said, 'Shush,' and they'd cease talking and lie for several more hours of inaction until dinner.

Once they came out of the water quickly due to the fact that she panicked when he tried letting go of her hands, and standing on the beach he stretched himself restlessly. All the strength and rest of days bunched in his shoulders. A fierce lustre in his green eyes. She thought she was about to lose him.

'I want white peaches that are imperishable,' she said, shivering. He looked down at her. He mistook her trembling for fear. He knelt and stroked her back in a round-and-round slow movement and said, 'The water won't harm you, baby.'

'It's not the water,' she said, and then he said, very thoughtfully, 'If I don't make you happy it's a waste of time.'

'But you do make me happy,' she said, leaning back on him. The rise and fall of his breathing deciding her own breaths. At times she thought her heart had gone behind his skin and his had entered her own, magically.

That night they went to another restaurant along the port at Cannes and she tasted another new fish.

'Twelve new fishes,' she said.

'Even Christ didn't have that variety,' he said. He looked at her laughing face, loose hair, honey-sweet glow on her neck, except where a gold chain kept a hair-line of white, a pendant between her fingers, the lips parted.

'You know something?' he said.

'What?'

'I'm going to save you for Sundays and Holy Days . . .'

'And I'll save you for weekdays,' she said. Her muscles ached from the swimming. Soon it would not be enough to

sit opposite and lie near and feel his heart beats through
her own. She wanted to die in him. He knew but hung
back from it. He kissed her each night at the bedroom
door and left until morning. Not in so many words but
with a look she would try to ensnare him.

'See ya . . .' he always said and went away. At times she
wanted him so badly she would have grovelled. On these
occasions she felt possessed by deep and agonizing humiliation. She must not degrade him. And yet he liked her and
it seemed so unnatural that he should not want to con-
summate his liking. He, the notable philanderer. The idea
that he might love her did not take grip because in some
ways she was not devoid of common sense. She had a
constant ache to be close to him. Under cover. The way
they were in the sea. But he always drew back. A resent-
ment slipped in between them when she tried to prolong
his kiss. Was she merely unattractive? He had loved
Denise. Ripe now and rosy all over with a heart like a
breaking rose, she wanted to lie under him and get from
him a child, quickly. She said it next night when they
were in a swish bar in Cannes. Always after dinner they
went to various bars for drinks. People looked at him,
waved, and sent drinks over, and still he gave everything
to her. He might look jokingly at the girls on stools poised
for discovery, but never long enough to alarm. She lived
in the world of his light-green eyes and his sudden mad-
ness and his equally sudden spasms of torture. Sometimes
he looked as if his body was being sawn through. She
thought he had a pain but he said no.

'I wouldn't want to hurt you,' he said, 'getting back to
the sleeping bit.'

'You wouldn't,' she said. 'I won't plague you tomorrow or the next day, I'll leave you alone.' She believed
this as she spoke it, because since her son she thought the
only valuable thing in the world is the gift of life. She

could cope with loss now, and a broken heart, and aloneness; she could cope with longing except when he sat
opposite her and trained the searchlight of his being on
hers. Her legs would automatically curve out and her
knees fall apart, surrendering. Her legs and the thighs
above them were like tree trunks frozen throughout a
winter until he had come, the God of Thaw, to flow
through the tree trunks of her legs and make it spring
again.

'But *I* might plague you,' he said.

'You won't.' He was going shortly, to make a picture,
and she was going home. Their paths, as she said half
jokingly, half solemnly, might never cross again.

'Drink up,' he said. They went to the next bar. They
liked to go to several each night. They were energetic and
wild and they loved to hustle into these quiet bars and
liven them for a bit, and also to revive themselves by the
newness of each place and the different sets of faces with
their very similar expressions, expressions hungry for fresh
adventures. He met up with friends whom he could not
ignore. Whole chains of people converged and put their
arms round his neck. He seemed to be a prodigal to them.
He drank a lot, and his eyes got quickly bloodshot. Again
she longed to bathe them with a little eye bath of soothing,
lukewarm liquid.

'Show ya . . .' a man said to him and took out a list of
telephone numbers. They were all girls' numbers. He
wanted Bobby to take a copy of the list. After each girl's
name there was a dossier:

'Mary, Mary must not be touched above knee.'

'Stella schoolteacher likes to come first.'

'Denise back from Austria on the 12th.'

But Bobby had these numbers. He took out his own
diary, read a telephone number, then another, and smiled!
They were the same numbers. Ellen walked out into the

lobby, she could not bear to listen. She kept walking up and down looking at scarves and blouses in the hotel display windows.

'You're full of shit,' she said when he came out. 'Of course,' he said. 'Did I ever say otherwise?' He linked her. They were going on to other night-clubs. Better spots.

'Where?'

'On . . .' His voice was very loud. She had a feeling that she should not go, that their days and nights were going to be fouled upon.

'I'll go back to the hotel,' she said.

'Don't do that.' He looked hurt. He was asking her to stay. She said she felt out of place. He cursed furiously. A whole string of ill-matching swear words flew from his lips, and above and beyond their resonant foulness she knew that he had called her a 'goodie-goodie'. She resented that and swore bitterly that she had never tried to thwart him in any way. One of his men friends came and asked what was going on, and shrugging it off Ellen followed them to the cars outside.

'We won't be too late,' she said. Bobby didn't answer. They went to a gambling place but she never got past the bar. Bobby and two other men disappeared for about an hour. She was among women who talked about the celebrities they knew and men who bought numerous drinks. Beautiful girls sat along the walls, patiently waiting for their gambling partners. If he didn't come within the hour she would go. Her mind was boiling over with vexation, but she tried to keep calm and centred her attention on a man who was contemplating a plate of sandwiches and who suddenly wrenched the beef from between the slices of bread and ate it with venom.

'Hello nurse.' Bobby came back to say he had lost a lot of money and would she mind waiting for a while until he retrieved some of it.

'You stay, I must go, I must go,' she said. She was tired and had drunk too much. The place frightened her. The people behaving like people in a slaughter-house, intent on only one thing: massacre.

'You won't stay?' He had collected an audience.

'I'm going.' She got off the high stool and moved shamefully towards the door.

'Okay, big nurse, you've been trying to bull it for weeks.' He followed her. His friends sniggered as they watched him catch hold of Ellen's shoulder. Out on the street he became contrite.

'I must stop it, I really must,' he said. 'I must get a shit detector.' She agreed. Such stupid people! Talking about celebrities and Thunderbird motor cars and jewelled watches.

'Even you,' she said.

'Even what?' he asked. He had the edginess of the drunk.

'Boasting about your wine cellar.'

'Don't even have one,' he said and brought her to the car. That night he did not conduct her to her own room but to the suite he had booked for himself in her hotel. She'd never set foot in it.

'My nurse,' he said and put his face to hers and kissed her as he had not kissed her before. They made love, of course. The sun that had passed into her limbs and through her old, bereaved bones came to life in her then and as they loved and struggled and fought and re-united she begged for him to thrust higher and higher and deeper and deeper because this time there was to be no mistake and nothing was to leak out of her. Afterwards she clung to him with her thighs and, extracting himself, it was as though he was now the breaking rose and his strength had fallen away inside her, like petals.

'Jesus,' he said. She could not understand him saying it.

'Are you shocked?' she said. He turned over and went to sleep. It was morning. Dawn glimmered through the half-shut blinds and light coldly entered the strange room. Unaccustomed as she was to a man she could not sleep with him beside her.

He wakened very soon after and got up. He was quite a while in the bathroom. Then he emerged, dressed.

'Where are you going?' she said, half out of bed now.

'To get a toothbrush,' he said.

'Use mine.' She would run down the corridor in his silk bathrobe and get one.

'Can't,' he said. 'My mouth's full of shit.' He went out.

She put it down to the remorse of the puritan, to hang-over, to moodiness, to exhaustion, but an hour later when he was not back she began to fret. She got up and went out and searched for him on the beach and along the other beaches and in the bars and she asked barmen but none of them had seen him.

'Last night, with a lady,' one man said.

'I know,' she said. He obviously didn't recognize her as the white-frocked creature of sanctity from the night before. At noon when she learnt that Bobby had settled his hotel bill, she took a car to Sidney's house. It was well into the mountains and the car got covered in dust. She kept looking at the dusty yellow chrome, as she stood at the hall door and waited. Antonio came and told her that Mr Bobby was not there and neither were any of the other guests. She asked where Mr Bobby might be. Antonio did not know. He asked if she would like coffee but she said no.

'Back to the hotel,' she said to the driver. It took about half an hour. They had an argument over the fare when they got back. He had quoted one price and asked for another.

'Crook,' she said. Luckily he didn't understand.

Chapter Sixteen

Two days later she found out. Too late to locate him, and anyhow, how could she be sure? It was a new situation and she was unfamiliar with the ethics. She reckoned that there was some sort of risk about accusing someone of having it, like there is in accusing someone of theft. She ground her teeth when she thought of him looking at the rim of dirt on his shirt-sleeve and saying 'Disgusting', and she thought if she had a good brother or a good male friend she would ask that good friend to go and kill him. But then again she remembered his reluctance and the shadow that came between them when she begged him to love her. Many of his jokes made sense now, and her anger was not that he had blemished her but that he had fled. He had not trusted her enough to stay. She thought, fondly for a minute, how they could get cured together. Do another joint thing. How long had he had it? Perhaps he didn't know himself. Perhaps it was contracted from Denise. At any rate it must have come to him from a woman and he gave it back to another woman: the perfect circuit of revenge. And at the same time she tried to dismiss it until that was no longer possible.

On the second day when she was lying on the mattress she felt a hot, burning pain. Hotter than the sun had ever made her. Putting her head between her knees, pretending to do a drawing on the sand, she sought out and confirmed the smell. It had been like that all night between her legs. Not the stealthy damp of nice desire but a scalding, unpleasant one. She took out a Cologne stick and touched her pulse and the back of her knees and her legs, and she thought, 'This will take it away, this cool anointment,' and she lay back and told herself it was all delusion, or the result of guilt. But by evening it felt worse and she hurried from the beach and put a chair to her bedroom door and took off her bathing suit to examine herself. There was no doubt. Something had infected her. The dark mesh of hair had a blight. She looked at it, smelt it, a nest of sobs now with ugly yellowing tears, and she damped the cake of soap and washed herself roughly as if by hurting herself she would take away her sin and her shame. Then she dried herself with her pants and wrapped them up in the English paper and put them on the bed until such time as she went out and could throw them in the sea. She foresaw herself contaminating the entire hotel, being found out, being asked to leave, a public scandal, the violinist running along behind her asking for compensation, with his notebook out also, getting the word and the symptoms. And then again she thought it could not be true. Perhaps it was the sun, or the salt water, or the pine cone she'd brought to bed the two nights since he left. The calm she thought she'd stored up from the five days with him had vanished. Even before she knew about the disease she had a desperate longing to be with him again. Down on the beach the sun no longer sustained her and she thought of everything he'd said and done, his jokes, his carelessness with money, the things he taught her and finally of his loving her, and she thought, 'I must hold something, someone, or I will die,' and she cradled her own body in her own arms. Then she saw the huge cone on the beach beside a coloured ball and she went over and picked it up. Its wings were opened and its colour grey from being continually washed by the sea. She held it and then brought it up to her room and put it on the chair beside her bed, and then she got so that she could not be still unless she held it, between her hands, between her legs, between the hollow of her breasts, in the folds of her arm, anywhere. Could this pine cone have done it, she thought, and looked again at the disgraced part where she'd just washed and knew with certainty that it would not stay dry and sweet-smelling for long. Already, despite the talcum, the smell was back in her nostrils, and taking the chair away from the door she put her hand on the service bell and waited with a wrap around her.

'I fear I have mislaid my T.C.P.,' she said when Maurice came.

'Madame,' he said beaming.

'For cuts,' she said, pointing to her wrist, where there were no cuts. She thought he sniffed. She drew back from him, petrified. She stood between him and the chair in the wrap, shivering. He thought she was merely cold.

'Soon is the time for lighting fires,' he said.

'Medicine,' she said frantically, and he grinned knowingly and said '*Oui*', and disappeared. He was back in a matter of minutes with a bottle of sweetened cascara and she almost threw it at him. Finally she escorted him to the room where the medical things were kept and she found some disinfectant and came back and put some on a pad and went out smelling of many different things, convinced that she would find a nice English doctor in whom she could confide.

'It's not a crime, it's not a crime, it's not a crime,' she kept saying, arranging her footsteps to tune in with that one sentence. 'It's not a crime,' she said again as she went through the hall and thought the manager looked very suspiciously at her. But even as she was saying it was not a crime she thought back to herself as a student nurse drawing away from the rich men who put their hands out to touch her black-stockinged knee that was on a level with the bed. How unsoiled she was then. The only one she indulged was the forester with the broken leg, who gave her gifts of pennies wrapped in paper. These he threw down when she went by the window to the nurses' quarters, to wash her hair and write a letter home, the ivory girl in her tower of gold. Would they recognize her now? It was as though she had fallen into a sewer. And yet she was able to look outside of herself, like a person going by, and say, 'This is not happening to me, it is all nightmare.'

She walked down the terrace of steps and crossed the road to walk under the trees, along the path that led to the town. Passing the church, she blessed herself and said, 'Oh God, grant I have not got syphilis,' before she said, 'Lord have mercy on his soul.' The two things uttered in the same breath shocked her. Even if the church were open she could not have gone in to pray. Farther down she stopped at the chemist's and bought four different bottles of disinfectant and some more talcum powder.

'Could you wrap them up?' she said. They produced a toilet bag, then a suitcase. They sold travel goods as well as medicines.

'Paper,' she said. It took several minutes to get a strong paper bag.

Outside it was warm. She'd put on a heavy skirt just in case and compared with everyone else she was dressed for Arctic weather. It was a tense night, the palm quills deathly still, motors going by, slowing down, whistles. A man whistled at her, but only to cover up for himself. Walking directly in front of her was a girl in gold lamé trousers and gold toplet who moved like a half-set jelly. Two cars had stopped for her at exactly the same moment. She got in the bigger car, and the other driver, not wanting to seem ignored, had propositioned Ellen.

'You wouldn't want to have anything to do with me, mate,' she said, bitterly.

'*Enchanté* . . .' he said.

She shook her head and crossed the road as if she were going to meet someone at the corner restaurant. The place where people met.

A clown performed and rode around on an old-fashioned bicycle, tempting death by swooping in and out in front of motor-cars, shaving their headlamps, getting squeezed between car doors, raising his hat to danger, making a squeak by pressing a toy that he had concealed under his arm; sometimes his legs were on the handlebars, sometimes his chest was. Just when he seemed to have escaped death he darted forward again in front of a speeding car and she heard the brakes screech, and she called out, 'Don't, don't,' and closed her eyes in case of something terrible. Nothing fatal. The car just overturned some tables, and the people, once they were over the shock, laughed again and the clown was safe. He saw her stand in terror and he rode in her direction madly, as if he was going to ride through her, then barely missing the tail of her heavy skirt he rode right into a bookshop and around the racks of books and magazines, jerking the handlebars. She drew into a side street while his back was turned.

In that street there were fewer people walking, but many sat at tables eating. It was the street where the eating was done, and later the people would move around to the main corner and watch the man on the bicycle and read the scraps of news on the neon lit ticker tape, and drink. She walked slowly past the tables, looking for an English doctor. She had no way of recognizing one but she thought that if someone fainted a doctor would come forward.

'Faint, faint,' she said, going by, being watched and watching; girls with measuring tapes checking on how much the meal had swollen their bellies, wine in lovely old-fashioned pitchers, and rosé in the ends of glasses specked with sediment. Every few yards a man – usually a young man – coming towards her, tried to engage her, first by walking directly in her path so that they would have to bump into each other, then when she side-stepped, by speaking to her, and finally by turning and following, until such time as she turned round and stamped her foot the way she might stamp her foot at a dog. That usually sent them away.

She passed a house with a brass plate nailed up outside, telling a doctor's name and the hours he was in attendance. It was encouraging to find it because if help did not come in the night she would rush round in the morning at the appointed hour. But help would come. She went into a lavatory and applied one of the new disinfectants. It looked strong, it burnt, that was a good sign. Maybe by the time she got back to her hotel the whole thing would have cleared itself. Her disease occupied her thoughts so much that she forgot Mark, and then when she remembered him she broke into sobs, but tearless sobs, and asked his forgiveness and said, 'This is only vinegar and gall.' She had no idea who she was speaking to, but all that night she talked to herself, blamed herself, hoped, pitied her ignorance and said, 'Doctor, Doctor, Doctor . . .' to match her footsteps. The thought of a hospital was too terrifying.

Quite by accident she came on the place that was canopied by the big tree where they went the night she had met the group, and she re-lived a little of it, Sidney as he dealt out the various packets of cigarettes like packs of cards and the mean people who pocketed the cigarettes straight away and the man with the fox tail between his legs and Gwyn with the big spotted handkerchief before her eyes.

'Gwyn,' she said out loud as if she just thought of a miracle, and she went into a quiet restaurant and drank a Pernod first and tipped enormously and then asked for the telephone. There was no telephone, so that she had to go to another restaurant and do exactly the same thing except that this time she made sure of the telephone before tipping. The waiter got the number for her and at the other end, Antonio – she was sure it must be he – asked her to hold on.

'Who is it?' Gwyn said, worried.

'Have I taken you from dinner?' Ellen asked, nervous.

'Who's that?'

'Ellen . . .'

'Oh, little Irish. Hello little old Irish, how are you?'

'I'm all right,' Ellen said, 'I didn't go home.'

There was a pause for a minute and she knew that Gwyn was thinking, 'What the hell.'

'We must have a get-together one evening, do I have your number?' Gwyn was saying now, rounding off the conversation.

'Gwyn,' Ellen said, 'do you remember what you said about having a friend?'

'Yes ma'am . . .'

'I'm in trouble . . .' Ellen said.

'Now that's not clever.'

'I know it's not.'

'Well you got to do something. How long is it gone? If you have your dates right it ought to be simple . . .'

'Gwyn,' Ellen said urgently, 'it's something else, worse than that. I got it while I was here . . .' There was a pause that seemed to be unending but must only have been minutes or the operator would have interrupted.

'You're not telling me you have the clap?' the woman said in a sharp, shocked voice.

'I have something,' Ellen said, looking down. There were ants all over the white plate that was left for the telephone money. She felt they would come inside her clothes and crawl around and nest and breed in her infected hair. She beckoned to the barman to bring her another drink.

'Hear that, Jason?' Gwyn said across the room, and her husband must have come across to the phone because Ellen could hear them murmuring and him saying, 'That's crazy,' and Gwyn saying, 'We must do something,' and him saying, 'No you don't,' and then at intervals Gwyn speaking into the mouthpiece and saying tonelessly, 'Just a minute,' she and him saying, 'A hot little broad like that, who the hell asked her to butt in?' and Gwyn saying, 'You're damn right,' but still telling Ellen to hold on. Finally she got the name of Sidney's doctor from Antonio and called it out and kept saying, 'Got that?' She spelt each word carefully.

'Can I say Sidney sent me?' Ellen said.

'Well it's not too swell a complaint, is it?' Gwyn said, and asked Jason what he thought.

'Huh,' Ellen could hear him say, 'don't ask me,' and then Gwyn went on with the doctor's address, but by that time Ellen had stopped writing it down.

Back in the hotel the manager waited for her. She went quite pale as he stood in the lobby and said,

'Madame Sage.'

Gwyn had telephoned, to warn him.

'Yes,' she said. She looked towards the tiny cubicles where the keys were. Her key was there.

'Please to come in,' he said and led the way to a small office at the back of the reception desk. She put the parcel behind her back. Was he going to examine her?

'Sit down, Madam,' he said. 'You are enjoying your stay?'

'Yes,' she said. 'My son died and I came here to get over it.' Nothing like pity. Was he a family man? No, he never married. He liked peace.

'Too bad about your son,' he said. He had a sallow,

gentle face, given to smiling. No matter what he said or she said, he smiled.

'What did you want?' she said. She might as well face it.

'Can I ask you somethink?' he said.

'Ask me,' she said, brazen now.

'There is a big beel,' he said. 'You are here twenty days.'

'Oh that,' she said, relieved.

'We like our guests to pay the fortnight, Madam, then we pay our bills and all is as perfect.'

'I'll pay it,' she said, leaning over, trying to read the amount. He had a sheet open in front of him.

'I will send it up,' he said.

'I'll pay it now,' she said, anxious to snatch it out of his hand and learn the amount. That smile was gluey.

'No, Madam, I will ask one of my boys . . .'

More tipping, she thought. She rose to go.

'You mix with nice people here?' he said.

'I mix with nice people,' she said, but he did not notice the bitterness.

'You have a lot of success on your trip,' he said.

'A lot,' she said. On the way to the door he held up a pair of glasses. 'You don't lose spectacles?' he said.

'No,' she said, and went upstairs to wait for the boy who was to bring her bill.

She put some more disinfectant on and then covered the various bottles with a napkin, just in case. She sat like someone sitting in wait for a death sentence. It came on a white dinner plate. There were thirteen pages in all. Typed on purple ribbon. She thought it a suitable colour in her state of mourning and uncleanliness. Quickly she skipped the typed pages and got to the last one to read the final amount.

It was far beyond the four-figure sum she had roughly reckoned on. She divided by twelve. Staggering. More than she had ever reckoned in her wildest calculations. Apart from the nightly fee of four pounds for her room, there were millions of incidental items. What could they be? She rang down and the manager told her there was an index at the bottom of each page, explaining what each charge was for. There were capital letters to denote whisky and laundry and ironing and Perrier and baths and cups of tea. The laundry and ironing and Perrier and baths and cups of tea were written first in French and then in English. She'd had hundreds of cups of tea. There was nothing for it but to sign all the travellers' cheques she possessed, and write out the balance on an ordinary cheque, then fly home and fling herself before her bank manager, begging for time to pay it back.

'Money decides everything,' she thought. Money would send her home when neither death nor disease could budge her. She wrote a cheque for more than the actual bill so that she would have a little French money for oddments until she left. But no more Perriers. She drank from the tap as if to invite typhoid and then went down carrying the bill on the plate. The manager said she should have rung. He would have sent a boy.

'Can you get a flight for tomorrow?' she asked.

'I will try,' and he picked up the telephone. He made a booking straight away. The season was fading, most of the people had gone home. He wrote down the time of the plane next day and she asked about a bus. He wrote down where she would get the bus and receipted her bill. Just as she walked away he called after her:

'Madam, I understant, the bill not right.'

'You overcharged,' she said, jubilant. She would have money back. She would buy a half-bottle of Pernod and forget the ire between her legs.

'Too small, we don't count tonight,' he said. She gave him back some of the notes he had given her in change and he handed her three franc pieces. She had fifty francs left and these three franc pieces. She was very broke.

Next day she tried to escape without being seen. She packed very quietly and ordered nothing so that Maurice need not come. About half an hour beforehand she closed the case and sat on the bed. The sunlight was bright in the room. She'd put two of the francs on an ashtray and kept the other in case a porter grabbed her baggage as she went through the hall. The thing had got worse. It was good that the money question had forced her to leave. She would see a doctor straight away, or go to a clinic. The name of a clinic was written up in a public lavatory in the centre of London. She would head for there.

''Bye,' she said to the room that contained so much of her. She'd taken two wooden hangers and one large towel with the hotel name on it. She put a towel in her travel bag just in case. She closed the door softly and moved along the corridor. The first to accost her was the man in charge of the bath. He tried to take her case but she held on to it. Then he put his hand out sullenly, and she walked by, a little laboriously, because of the heavy case. Down in the lobby it was calamitous. Maurice, the waiter from her table, and another boy were sitting on a bench inside the door. They all leapt up to assist her. Maurice had his hand on the leather strap of the case. Did she want taxi?

'No, no,' she said, but did not look at him at all. To the boy who was last in the row she gave the one franc and hurried on, down the concrete slope towards the trees and the bus terminal, running now that she had made her escape. It was hot and fiery and bright. But she knew that when she remembered the place it would not be hot like that but as it was the first night she came: blue and unknown, about to deliver up to her the most poignant experience of her life. And maybe it had.

Chapter Seventeen

At home the hall was strewn with letters and there were two telegrams. Some of the letters had been posted and some were delivered by hand. They were all messages of sympathy. She had more friends than she ever dreamed. She opened several at once, scanned them, looked down to their signatures and thought how considerate people were. Some had even gone to the trouble of getting paper and envelopes edged with black. Although in fact this type of paper nauseated her. There were two from her boss. The first was full of condolence, the second was still sympathetic but mainly said, 'Where are you?' The first telegram was from Hugh Whistler and it said:

WHAT CAN I DO TO HELP

The second was from him too and it said:

PLEASE RING ME, PLEASE

It had been sent by mistake on a greetings form. It was strange, holding them together, the letters with their thick black edging and the telegram decorated with pink rosebuds. She shivered; the letters did not distract her enough. She had to make the journey to his bedroom. She ran to get it over with. His fort and soldiers were laid out on the floor and the pile of clean clothes on the bed where she'd left them, after ironing. She thought, 'If I cry now I'll never stop.' She just picked up the clothes and put them in a bureau drawer and then she walked out of the room and turned the key in the door. She busied herself looking at the rest of the house, seeing if everything was as she left it. The garden was in a bad way. The geraniums dead in their pots. She felt the clay. Like cement it was. She got out the hose and went up and down the garden training the water on the flower-beds, the rockeries, and even on the dead geraniums. The garden seemed to breathe again and the earth crumbled as the water soaked through.

After a while she thought of her husband, although in fact he had been in her mind constantly. She washed herself most carefully and took a long time over it. She had got into the habit of washing over and over again as if there was some way of erasing it. She put on a dark dress and set out for her husband's house around six. It was bright, of course, but not the fierce white brightness she had become accustomed to. It was a softer country; she would talk to him and say how awful it was, for him, for her, for anyone forced to live with an incurable sorrow. On the bus she missed her child more than anywhere. They had made that same journey so often, especially at week-ends when she delivered him to his father's gate. They usually swopped riddles. She thought if they produced another child he might be the same. Reproduce their son exactly. But then she thought of her other trouble and felt daunted. She dimly knew that diseases like that were hereditary and the sins of the parent were truly visited upon the child. Her husband would have her publicly stoned if he knew. In fact she would have to be careful and keep several yards away from him in case he detected anything. She should have gone to a doctor first, not that she felt confident about going to a doctor at all.

The house looked very quiet, the hedge had grown wild in the month and the windows were boarded up. She rang and looked through the letter box and called. He'd put an old chamois inside the box so that she could not see through. Perhaps he'd died in there. She knocked at a neighbour's door. They were semi-detached houses, divided by thin walls, and the neighbour would know if he was stirring around inside. The neighbour said he had not been there for days. He had gone away. He'd carried out some things – books, a clock and a record player – one day and put them in the car and driven off. There was a girl with him.

'A nice girl?' Ellen said foolishly.

'In her twenties I would say,' the woman said. 'She had her hair down her back.'

For an instant Ellen felt the old repetitive stab: she too had had her hair down on her back when they met; and then something happened to change that feeling because suddenly she felt tears come in her eyes but they were tears of relief. Out of his pillaged life he had the strength to start afresh, to lay his head on some pure green breast where the milk might be wholesome. She was thankful to him in some strange way. He had freed her of the responsibility of feeling eternally guilty for him. More than anything she wished that they should be happy, he and this strange girl. She couldn't bear the thought of it being just a girl who came to rent the house or deliver a breakable parcel to him. Maybe they fell in love at first sight. Maybe. Maybe. Maybe. Curiosity had died in her. For the first time she felt a fierce indifference. The passing away of the child and the boarded-up house put finality to their marriage. No more torture. In time he would write, but the letter would be about formalities and her reply would be businesslike too.

'Is the house for sale?' she asked the neighbour.

'Not that we know of,' the neighbour said, frantic to ask questions, eyeing Ellen's body as if there was something to be learnt from it.

'Will you let me know if it is?' Ellen said, and gave her office telephone number. There was a set of old teaspoons in there she wanted. Her key to the house was no use because he had the locks changed after she left him. The teaspoons were all she coveted now, although when she left him she had tried to get back in and read his mind by the memos he wrote for himself on calendars, by the number of dirty cups on the table, by the squashed state of cushions in chairs. That was all behind her. The teaspoons were a different matter. They were silver, but that was not the point, because they were dented. Her mother had sent them as a wedding present, although she'd fallen out with her daughter for marrying a heathen. She sent the gift and put no name to it. Her mother had stolen them from the big house where she worked, because the initials were there for all to see, and Ellen thought it a very noble thing for her mother to have done. An actual gift. This was all she wanted from her early life, and she would have liked one pleasant photograph of her husband and of course the child's belongings. Fragments were enough: in time those people who had meant everything to her and consumed her thoughts and inflamed her passions, those same people would become fragmented too and days would go by and she would not think about any of them. Her son would be the last to be relinquished but he would go, just as he would have gone of his own volition, if he had lived. Life had rendered her down: she no longer cherished any illusions about everlasting love, or about steadfastness.

'Just a couple of odds and ends I wanted to pick up,' she said.

'Of course, it's only natural, every woman has her souvenirs,' the neighbour said. But the look in her eye was saying, 'Your son is dead and you're still alive, what a heartless woman you must be.'

'And of course I have to arrange for a tombstone,' Ellen

said, taking offence at the woman's unspoken thoughts. She had already decided on a rock, a strong, jagged rock the colour of blue slate. In a week or two she would take a train down there, and if she found his father had arranged for anything different she would have to usurp those arrangements. A rock was the most fitting thing for a young grave. A rock would outlast them all. And no inscription. Nothing soppy.

'Of course, the poor little chap,' the neighbour was saying. 'His ball came over the hedge one day, and he asked ever so . . .'

Ellen had to go. With a sudden bolting move she excused herself. The neighbour must have thought her very callous. Yes, she was callous, she was hurrying away to find a doctor to cure herself. Already Bobby meant nothing, he had merely been the bearer of infection. The three-wise-men fable in reverse. Not that she blamed him. Blame, like nostalgia, was a sensation she had dispensed with. Trivial, all of these tags, when set against the huge accident of being alive or not. The days on the beach were some spent dream, only her disease was real, and the air around her and the stones of the road, and cars going by.

The neighbour closed the door hurriedly. Probably ran to tell her husband the news.

Why Ellen rang Hugh Whistler she was never sure. It certainly was not to start up anything romantic. On the telephone she thanked him for both telegrams, and hearing his voice she thought how English and formal and uninspired he was. She felt the same sort of relief as she had experienced outside her husband's over-grown home. She no longer cared about whom he loved or whom he saw, she had no need of him, no innuendo slipped into the conversation, she simply answered drab questions and asked others. It was a new sensation, indifference; it was like observing a party as one passed by a sleek and softly lit front room and having no feeling of regret about being uninvited because to walk the streets alone provided a greater and surer pleasure.

'Perhaps through the week,' she said. He was asking when they could meet. She dallied. He insisted on visiting her later that night when his newspaper was put to bed.

She could see that her rude glow of health shocked him. When he looked at her face, he gasped. And the whites of her eyes! That clear pale-blue of baby's eyes.

'It's all out of bottles, sun lotion, rouge, belladonna, everything . . .' The apology wrung from him a smile.

'It was terrible,' he said as he kissed her cheek.

'It is terrible,' she said. Between the time she came back from her husband's house and waited for him the hours had been savage. She went around and beat upholstered chairs with her fists and knocked her forehead against various walls hoping to knock herself unconscious.

'How are you?' she said. He looked pale, aged. It did not take long to learn why. His girl friend had left. Another man. His double really.

'When will men and women get used to being alone?' she said.

'She resented my children,' he said and was off on some long story about how his children came for breakfast once a month and two of them fancied hot milk on their cereal but she insisted they have cold milk.

'Wouldn't take the trouble to heat it,' he said.

'Perhaps she thought it might kill the vitamins,' Ellen said, not so much to defend the woman but because she'd taken to finding numerous rational reasons for the most absurd behaviour. He looked at her startled. Since when had she become so matter of fact? Then, remembering his duties as a mourner, he said,

'Do you want to tell me about it?'

He was on the edge of the chaise, totally ill at ease, not

163

even drinking the whisky she had given him. It was strange to see his beautiful face again and know that what once thrilled and stirred her now only created a void. As if she had become another person. He patted the blue velveteen beside him and asked her to sit.

'I'll sit here,' she said. She could not trust herself to be close to him because of the other matter.

'You would be more at ease in my arms.'

To that she closed her eyes nervously and started sniffing to make sure there was no odour. At least the whisky smell was all pervasive.

'I wouldn't,' she said. Her monstrous affliction had put her out of the reach of other people. It was funny to think that insanity was the downfall that used to dog her, of how she might go raving mad like the two women who thrust themselves into the solitary lake. But this was something less pitiful; contagious, and unforgivable in fact. Nothing moved or spoke to her from the real world now unless she saw in it an echo of her own cast-away plight. There could be no chance that anyone would want to help her, any more than she had helped her own son. Fate. Or, created by herself, and her own wilful follies. Either way these things had all happened and were float-ing under her memory's eye and would be sealed eventu-ally by her death. Dumb and insensible to the call of friendship, sex, whisky, comfort, she could only contain herself by repeating to herself that there were in the world strangers, doctors, science, drugs – things that could cure her body at least. She thought of the Confessional and that black grille through which she used to murmur 'I cursed, I told lies, I had bad thoughts', and she remem-bered that she never came away feeling absolved no matter how great the priest's strictures had been or how painful the penance. Perhaps it was the same with bodily ailments. Her stomach still bore the pitter-patter marks of muscles strained in childbearing, and a neck operation had left a permanent scar. Nothing healed.

'You would,' he said, 'because I want you more than the last time I saw you.'

The words couldn't have surprised her more. She opened her eyes and smiled on him.

'You don't believe it,' he said. She thought back to their long day together, their vigil over the wall, the hours in bed, their wet, contented, joined-together bodies and how she'd yearned about his going away, wanting it almost as much as she dreaded it. How nice it would be to snuggle down with him and feel newly warm and welcome it for its own brief passing sake rather than as a life investment. Impossible! Her eyes brimmed with tears. The first in weeks.

'What is it?' he said. He put his hand out, sweetly and gently, to steer her from the high-backed chair to the place next to him on the velveteen chaise. A nest. But she dare not risk it. She had washed before he came, but it was still chancy. Also she found that in tense situations it became worse, as if she were crying down there. Across the room, while she sobbed a bit, he talked about many things: the weather, the editorial he had written that night, the kind of car he planned to buy in the autumn. But he kept coming back to it, to them, to his need for her to sit close to him.

'I thought about you,' he said. 'Not just because your son got killed, but about . . . everything.' She looked at his pale, earnest face. His tongue moistened his top lip, it was a habit of his. She had not thought of him once. Not once. That was her crime. Under the soft skin and behind the big, melting eyes, her heart was like a nutmeg. Some of it had been grated by life but the very centre never really surrendered to anyone, not to the mother who stole for her, nor to the drunken father, nor to her far-seeing but poisoned husband, and not to the child in the way it should have. No wonder she clung to the parable about white peaches.

'You know what I want,' she said. He came and knelt near her and gave her the cigarette he had just lit. She drew her dress farther down over her legs and curled those legs under the chair, shrivelling away from him.

'I'm not going to rape you,' he said. 'I would only make love to you.'

'You know what I want,' she said again. 'To cease to be me.'

He said nonsense, that she was one of the sweetest girls he ever met. The mean joys of vanity possessed her for a moment and then she stopped listening to him and said, to herself, 'I want to love someone or something, so utterly, and to ask for nothing in return and to die for loving that thing if necessary.' He crushed her hands, asked her to come back to him, say something.

'I want to love someone other than myself,' she said.

'We all do that a little,' he said. He was such a flat person to talk to.

'Pure love.' It sounded pompous, and she drank from the whisky glass to give some ordinariness to the occasion.

'It's your Roman Catholicity,' he said.

'It's how I feel,' she said flatly. Then smiled. He put his face to her hands and kissed them and looked at them as if he was looking at a clump of flowers.

'Don't,' she said. She kept backing into the chair.

'Is it because of his death?' he said.

'No, I slept with everyone in France, tinker, tailor, soldier, sailor . . .' she said, as much to flagellate herself as to disillusion him.

'You poor girl,' he said, because of course he did not believe her. 'I must decide for us both.'

'You can't decide for me, no one can,' she said. He got

himself another drink, he walked around, he stood behind her chair and embraced her. She thought, 'If he finds out by coming near me he will shun me for ever.' Every time he touched her she felt he was coming nearer to finding out her shame.

'Hugh,' she said, not having to look at him because he was behind her, 'you'll have to go.'

'You want me to go?' he said.

'Yes.'

She felt him move and heard him put the glass down. He picked up his lighter and his tie which he'd taken off because the night was so warm.

'Maybe in a month or two, or at Christmas, we'll make candles,' she said, trying to be cheerful. He took the packet of French cigarettes and pushed back the ones that had fallen out and put them in his pocket.

'Can you leave me a cigarette for the morning?' she said. He left the whole packet.

'Only one,' she said.

'I'll get some when I go out,' and he gave a little smile of forgiveness. He was handsome. And not impatient. And there were as many lovable girls in the world as there are stars in the December sky. The futility of what was happening seemed to take her by the throat. And the irony. She felt she might be sick and she had only one idea: to get him out, to wash herself again and again and see it through.

Within a few days she rang a friend who put her on to a nice lady doctor in a very exclusive part of outer London. There was a little fur mouse as a mascot on the doctor's table and Ellen sat eyeing the mouse and telling her story as calmly as she could. She felt inhibited.

'This is not your husband.'

'No, it *was* not my husband.'

The lady doctor made notes and took records: her age, her pregnancy, her present symptoms, and then sat her on the couch. Always at the prospect of being medically examined she cried. This time was no exception, and her limbs tightened.

'Well if you must be careless you've got to pay,' the lady doctor said grimly as she probed first with a rubber-gloved finger and then with a cold metal instrument. It hurt. In all she did seven tests and by the end of the examination Ellen was quite reconciled to having seven different diseases. Except that she would not know for a few days. Meanwhile at work she wore heavy skirts and two pairs of knickers to insulate herself.

On her second visit she sat once again beholding the mouse and the grim little fat-chested woman.

'I've had a letter,' the woman said, holding it. 'And it appears there is a secondary infection, but no gonorrhoea infection . . .'

'After all my worrying,' Ellen said. She felt a bit cheated but relieved all the same. In fact for a minute there was a danger that she might have done something disgraceful like clapping. She got a prescription for pills and a violet lotion, and going out she thought gladly how the lotion would stain all her pants and the stains in themselves would be a testimony of mourning. Ugly irregular purple shapes.

She walked part of the way home across a common, holding the medicine parcel tight. The birches were turning, their leaves like sovereigns. Tufts of rough grass sprouted ochre, the ground beneath was a worn, faded yellow, the light in the air mellow. She had been walking fast. She stopped herself and stood: no need to hurry now, nothing to hurry to, she breathed, not happy, not unhappy – if the days were never to be quite so lustrous-bright again, equally so the nights would not be as black. Or so she liked to think. Leaves fell, she watched them drop off, curl down and lodge in a bed of grass, still heavy with moisture, they were falling all around her, simple and unceremonious; for a month or two at least, a cool and lovely autumn.

More about Penguins and Pelicans

Penguinews, which appears every month, contains details of all the new books issued by Penguins as they are published. It is supplemented by our stocklist, which includes almost 5,000 titles.

A specimen copy of *Penguinews* will be sent to you free on request. Please write to Dept EP, Penguin Books Ltd, Harmondsworth, Middlesex, for your copy.

In the U.S.A.: For a complete list of books available from Penguins in the United States write to Dept CS, Penguin Books, 625 Madison Avenue, New York, New York 10022.

In Canada: For a complete list of books available from Penguins in Canada write to Penguin Books Canada Ltd, 2801 John Street, Markham Ontario L3R 1B4.

Margaret Drabble

A Summer Bird-Cage

Two sisters. Bright, attractive Sarah, newly down
from Oxford; and beautiful Louise, married to the
rich but unlikeable novelist Stephen Halifax.
Despite a promising start things seem to be going
badly and, as the situation builds to its bizarre
climax, Louise and Sarah have to discover whether
they can forgive each other for existing.

The Millstone

Rosamund – independent, sophisticated, enviably
clever – is terrified of true maturity. Then, ironically,
her first sexual experience leaves her pregnant . . .

The Garrick Year

This novel takes the lid off a theatrical marriage;
inside we find Emma, married to an egocentric
actor playing a year's season at a provincial theatre
festival, David, her husband – and Wyndham
the producer. The mixture turns rapidly to acid.

Jerusalem the Golden

The girl from Northam was grateful to find herself
accepted in London intellectual circles. She could
become the golden girl and have real affairs with
married men, just like in the novels.

The Waterfall

Jane Gray, poetess and failed wife, considered herself
a disaster area. Until the husband of her alter ego,
cousin Lucy, climbed into her bed. With her
customary insight into feminine psychology
Margaret Drabble peels away the defensive layers
of self-deception, guilt, and compromise with which
women protect their sensitive, vulnerable core.

Also published
The Needle's Eye
The Ice Age

Joan Didion

Play It As It Lays

Maria Wyeth is thirty-one years old and alone on the Hollywood freeway driving fast to nowhere. Behind her, the familiar debris of a failed contemporary life: a marriage, a divorce, a child in a mental home, a 'clean' abortion, a short career as a film star. Ahead of her – in a world where there are 'rattlesnakes under every rock' and human beings seem unable to help or even touch each other – what?

Slouching Towards Bethlehem

Joan Didion delivers her verdicts on The Great American Way of Life . . . Her title essay, describing the hippies of San Francisco, reflects her main theme: 'that things fall apart'. And, among other subjects, she reports on Joan Baez, looks wryly at John Wayne, airs her views on morality, analyses California and Hawaii and pauses for a searching backward glance into her youth.

Run, River

Lily couldn't cope with people even before her father and Rita drowned. But when her husband Everett goes to the war, and his father has a stroke, and his sister Martha becomes impossible, her desperate need for love engulfs them all in an emotional whirlpool. And finally, Lily is the only one left, floating helplessly with the currents.

A Book of Common Prayer

'All I know now is that when I think of Charlotte Douglas . . . I am less and less certain that this story has been one of delusion.'

Charlotte arrives in Boca Grande at the end of two marriages, grieving over a daughter turned bomb-throwing revolutionary. Into the white, glaring heat she carries her luggage of clean-cut American expectations which promise her that the world is full of others like herself – or does she?

Edna O'Brien

A Scandalous Woman

'All the essence of the O'Brien craft is distilled here' –
Evening Standard

The eight short stories of this collection have a dual theme;
Ireland – its people, its personality, and Woman – woman
betrayed, or sacrificed, innocence involuntarily lost,
happiness stolen or mislaid.

Edna O'Brien has concentrated on the discovery and
perfection of despair: she fixes on those vivid moments
when a child first understands she is not valued, when
a wife suddenly sheds all grace, or an old woman makes
up her mind to loneliness.

'Unambiguously, aggressively alive' – *Observer*

'Her new collection of stories is one of the best things she
has done' – *Sunday Telegraph*

Edna O'Brien

The Country Girls
This famous first novel introduces two delightful
heroines, Kate and Baba, and a host of other
Irish characters in unpredictable situations.

Girl with Green Eyes
The comic and poignant sequel to *The Country Girls*
in which Caithleen Brady finds romance in Dublin.

Girls in their Married Bliss
Readers of the previous two novels will not be
surprised at the tragicomedy of the married lives of
Kate and Baba.

Casualties of Peace
Willa had loved and been hurt by love so she tried
to shut out the threat of feeling.

The Love Object
The heroine of each of these short stories swings in
her different way between euphoria and agonizing
disappointment.

Night
Through one long night Mary Hooligan speaks – her
thoughts, feelings, loves; her history.

A Pagan Place
In a stream of image, impression, expression, experience
and bitter fact of life, Edna O'Brien catalogues
the almost delicious agony of the poor Irish child.

Zee & Co
Edna O'Brien explores the sexual geometry of the
eternal triangle – and discovers some acute new
angles . . .